QUEEN OF NIGHT
AND THE WITCH OF
WESTCHESTER

"If you have an idea, that you genuinely think is good—DON'T LET SOME IDIOT TALK YOU OUT OF IT."

—Stan Lee

Queen of Night and the Witch of Westchester

Cover Design by Sajal Kumar Chand
Interior Formatting by Brady Moller

First Edition
ISBN: [979-8-9999599-0-4]

Printed in the United States of America

For more information, visit:
[Instagram: @Thebeasleynetwork] [Email: Thebeasleynet@gmail.com]

QUEEN OF NIGHT

AND THE WITCH OF
WESTCHESTER

MICHAEL BEASLEY

Contents

I'd like to dedicate this book to my mom and dad, and to all of my supporters. To the small but mighty Queen of Night fanbase. Don't wait for the perfect moment.

if they don't give you the keys to the castle, build your own empire—brick by brick and soon enough, you'll make enough noise where they'll come to you.

I would also like to dedicate this book to the little boy who was in speech therapy as a kid and went on to speak in front of thousands of people. To the young man who did not know his own worth, and walked through the valley, and came out the other end as— the 'Best in the World'.

"First love never dies... but this time—it kills."

Chapter
ONE

THE LOVERS

To outsiders, The Bronx is considered a dangerous place, and it is, just not for the reasons they think. Little does anybody know, true evil lurks in the shadows, and if you look for it, it'll be sure to find you. Few are courageous enough to venture into the darkness, and even fewer are able to make it out alive. And here I am brave enough to tell you its secrets.

It was just another Friday night in The Bronx. The streets were buzzing with young adults enjoying the mild weather—warm enough to stay out, with a cool breeze hinting that Autumn was near. Music from different genres blared from all directions, with reggaeton, bachata, hip hop, and the occasional police siren in the mix. Like most urban neighborhoods, some spots were sketchy, but as long as you didn't look lost or like you were up to no good, you could enjoy your weekend without trouble. Despite the lively streets, I was at my own kind of party.

I stood with my back against the wall at my friend Ricky's birthday party, held in the basement of his aunt's apartment building, in a room meant for events like this. I wasn't really into parties, but if someone invited me, I'd make an effort to show up and support them. Ricky's 21st birthday was set to be the biggest party of the year, and since he was team captain of Lehman College's baseball team last year, spreading the word was easy.

The party room was packed with college students and Ricky's family, all dancing, drinking, and vibing to Latin hip hop. I wasn't a big fan of Spanish music. I didn't speak much Spanish either, just the basics I picked up in high school to get by. Even though I felt out of place, I stayed and swayed my shoulders a bit, trying to look like I was enjoying the music. Now, if they'd played some hip hop, I'd be rapping along like I wrote the lyrics myself.

Two people in the crowd caught my eye.

To my left was my good friend Milly, who I'd brought to the party with me. She wasn't a college student and didn't know anyone else there, but Milly had a knack for making friends with strangers in minutes and dancing with them like no one was watching—which she eventually did. That was just Milly. She had this aura that made both men and women fall for her. She was only 5'3" and currently in her red hair phase.

I know what you're thinking—why don't I ask her out? I'm getting there. Our relationship is interesting. We grew up together; she used to live right next door until she moved in with her sister at 16. Now she's just a couple of blocks away. To be honest, I had a major crush on her when we were younger. I basically loved her at one point, and she knew how I felt back then.

In my tween years, I'd ask my mom for money to buy her flowers and chocolates for Valentine's day. I even wrote her poetry, as best as a thirteen year old could, but I never shared it, worried it might make her uncomfortable.

My favorite moments with her were when it was just the two of us sitting on the staircase in our apartment building. We'd talk for hours, and no matter what was going on in my life, time stood still when I was with her. Hearing her laugh made my day, and every hug from her recharged me, like I could carry the weight of the world until the next time she wrapped her arms around me. I know, I was such a sap.

To make a long story short, there came a point as teenagers when she seemed worried that I might still have feelings for her. I didn't want to risk losing the joy she brought into my life. So, despite my feelings, we stayed friends. I had to bury those feelings, grow up, and accept that she didn't see me the way I wished she did.

After all these years, Milly and I are polar opposites in how we see and navigate the world, yet I would say we made great teammates. We balanced each other out.

To my right, the other person who stood out in the crowd was Jessica. She was chatting with her friends, holding a red cup in her hand. I took a moment to admire her beauty from afar.

Jessica was beautiful, but in some ways, she was a lot like me. She was an introvert, yet everyone knew and liked her. She was smart, hardworking, and ambitious, and we even shared the same major—Journalism!

Our history wasn't as deep as mine and Milly's, but there was something special about Jessica that drew us together over the past year. Out of all the girls I've dated or been attracted to, Jessica is the only one who could rival Milly in making me feel something truly deep.

Jessica lifted her head and slowly locked eyes with me, as if magnets were pulling us together. Without thinking, I gave a small smile and raised my empty red cup to her, nodding. Through the darkness and flashing strobe lights, I caught the glow of her smile in return. The music was playing, but all I heard was muffled sounds. Then, I felt a shift inside me, like my subconscious was urging me to turn to my left. Before I could, a familiar voice snapped me out of my gaze.

"D'Angelo!" Milly said sharply, snapping me back to reality. The atmosphere resumed, and the world seemed to return to balance. The anxiety that had crept into me had vanished as quickly as it came.

"Yeah? Hey, are you okay?" I asked.

"Yeah, I'm good—just a little tipsy and tired," she replied with a slight, charming smile.

"Oh, okay. Just checking. I see Ricky's enjoying himself."

We both glanced over our shoulders and saw Ricky, the birthday boy, dressed in all-white formal attire, singing along and dancing to the reggaeton music. You couldn't miss him—he was a 6'3, semi large Dominican guy wearing a crown.

Milly looked back at me and giggled.

"Yeah. Don't you want to dance?"

"Oh, um, no thanks. I'll sit this one out," I replied, even though I'd been sitting most of them out anyway.

"How about you?" I asked. "You don't wanna dance anymore?"

"I feel a little—"

I couldn't hear her over the loud music.

"Huh?" I said, leaning in slightly.

"I said I was—"

At this point, the music got louder, and I could only see her mouth moving without hearing her words. The music, now pretty catchy, was all I could hear.

"What!" I shouted.

Milly gave me a look of defeat and frustration. She grabbed my wrist and dragged me toward the exit. As we approached, I locked eyes with a guy standing by the door. He patted me on the shoulder and gave me a thumbs-up.

I smiled in confusion, wondering why he was so happy to see me when I didn't even know him. Then it hit me, and I laughed to myself.

Milly led me into the narrow basement hallway, lit only by a single bright light near the party room doors. The ends of the hallway faded into darkness. The music was quieter here, making it easier to hear.

"I said I was feeling a little weird," she said firmly, in a hushed tone.

"Why, what happened?" I asked.

"Nothing, I just felt like some guys were staring at me."

"Well, can you blame them?" I said jokingly.

Milly is no stranger to getting attention from guys, and I'm no stranger to seeing it. Sometimes, a guy or even a girl doesn't take the hint that she's not interested, and that's where I come in. Usually, just my presence is enough to steer them away.

After standing up to her abusive boyfriend when I was only 16, confronting strangers became easier. He was several years older and possessed a larger build compared to me. He didn't hurt me, but I remember the feeling of accepting the possibility that he could. They didn't last long, thankfully. But none of the people she had desired would be worth bragging about either. At least none that I've seen.

Maybe I was only brave because I was defending Milly; I certainly didn't have that same bravery when I was bullied in ninth grade.

"I'm serious, D'Angelo," she said with a smile. "But it's whatever. Does everyone here go to college?"

"Yeah, it's Ricky's birthday party, so he invited a lot of people from our college. Other than that, it's mostly his friends and family," I explained.

"Oh, okay. I'm going to step outside. It's getting a bit hot, and I need some fresh air," she said, beginning to fan herself with her hand.

I was concerned about us separating. If I followed her, I might come off as clingy, but if I didn't, something might happen to her. I'm no party expert, but I know you're supposed to look after your friends at events, especially those you came with. Before I could protest, I reminded myself that I had my cell phone on me in case she needed me. Still, my gut told me to ask if she wanted me to come along.

"Okay, do you want me to come with you?" I asked.

The music in the party room changed, and the crowd cheered. Milly glanced over her shoulder at the door leading back to the party. She spun back to me and flashed a smile.

"No, no! I'm good, really. Enjoy yourself!" she said, lightly caressing my right bicep.

I watched her leave, navigating through the dark hallway and squeezing past the crowd blocking the staircase. As she disappeared from view, my stomach clenched, until the sudden sound of a metal doorknob turning from the party room caught my attention.

Ricky, in his flamboyant style, burst through the double doors, took a deep breath, and savored the quieter tone of the hallway. With satisfaction written across his face, we exchanged a dap handshake and a brotherly hug.

"What's up, D'Angelo!?" he hollered.

"I'm good," I replied. "How's it going, man? And hey, Happy Birthday again!"

"Thanks! I'm good, you shhh-know?" You could tell Ricky was in a good mood when his Bronx accent came out. "But what about you, man? Was that the girl you were talking about?"

"Yeah, that's Mills," I said.

I only mention Milly to my closest friends, usually in conversations about our love lives. While my friends were aware of other girls I was interested in, they all knew about the "myth and legend" that is Milly. If they ever met her, it would be like meeting a celebrity or a unicorn. Fortunately, Ricky already knew the details of where Milly and I stood, but like everyone else, he couldn't resist asking the age-old question whenever the opportunity arose.

"Oh cool, you gonna make your move, though?" he asked playfully.

"Nah, I told you, we've been friends for years. I'm deep in the friend zone," I explained. "Besides, you know I have a thing for Jessica."

"Oh, right, right! So you're finally going to make a move on Jessica?"

I love my friends; they always believe in me, even when I don't believe in myself. They know I move at my own pace. Unfortunately, if I stick to my usual speed, things might never get done. At least I'm self-aware.

"Oh, well, yeah, someday," I muttered. But before I could come up with some lame excuse, Ricky had interjected.

"Oh no, no, no, D'Angelo, listen to me. You're an awesome dude," he said, draping his arm over my shoulders. His heavy arm guided me back to the party room. With a single swing of his free hand, he threw open the door, and I was hit by the thumping bass of the party's speakers. The loud music didn't stop Ricky from giving me his brotherly advice.

"But you have to take chances!" Ricky urged. "You never know what might happen! So go out there and get what you want, man!"

Without warning, Ricky gave me a playful push. It was light enough not to hurt but firm enough to send me into the crowd.

I bumped into someone and turned to apologize. But before I could say a word, I recognized the deep brunette curls. I paused, taking in the girl behind the beautiful hair. Jessica turned and greeted me with a wide, pearly white smile that stretched from ear to ear.

"Oh, I'm so sorry!" I exclaimed.

"Hey D'Angelo! It's okay! How are you?" she called out.

"I'm good, thanks! Just celebrating Ricky's birthday!"

"Same!" she giggled.

Sometimes, saying something obvious can come off as cute rather than stupid—at least, that's what I'll call it for now. We shared an awkward nod in unison. *Time for the one-two punch*, I thought.

"You look really—great!"

Smooth.

"Thank you! You too!" she replied, flashing her award-winning smile.

A burst of guitar notes from the speakers filled the room with energy, and the crowd around us buzzed with excitement. I wasn't familiar with most Hispanic music, but this one was recognizable. It was "Dile al Amor" by Aventura. I'd played this classic a few times in my room, pretending to know the lyrics and what the song was really about. My high school Spanish grade of 70 only told me it was a love song. I think.

Jessica tilted her head and looked to the side, grinning as if lost in a deep thought. I watched, eager to see her next move. Part of me hoped she wouldn't ask what I feared, while another part hoped she would. With wide, excited eyes, she turned back to me.

"Wanna dance?" she asked.

Lightning seemed to strike through my body. My heart skipped a beat. Hello, anxiety. I started to wonder if anyone else felt as dizzy as I did. *Say something, you idiot!*

"Um—sure, but I'm not really good at it," I muttered. I thought it was fair to warn her and give her a chance to back out if she wanted. But my warning didn't faze her.

"It's fine," she said with a smile. "I'll show you!"

So far, this night felt like being tossed around on a life raft in the middle of the ocean. But for the first time, the pull was gentle, graceful, and reassuring. The waves calmed, the clouds parted, and a ray of sunshine seemed to shine down on me. This new territory felt unfamiliar, but I knew I was safe—and better yet, I wasn't alone.

Her soft hand brushed against mine as she raised it to our side. She closed the gap between us, stepping closer and giving me a warm smile. Instinctively, I placed my right hand on her lower back while she rested her hand on my shoulder. I felt a lump in my throat but pushed it aside. Now wasn't the time to overthink. I tucked my chin and focused on her shoes.

She began taking three side steps to the left, swaying her hips to the beat. I followed her lead, trying to match her rhythm while avoiding too much hip movement. We switched to stepping right, repeating the same steps. It wasn't rocket science—just bachata. As we moved back and forth, I glanced up and saw her already looking at me, her eyes conveying a warm invitation. I couldn't help but return her smile, feeling a silent encouragement: *You've got this!*

For once, I didn't second-guess myself. I tightened my grip on her hand, spun her around, and added a bit more flair to my steps. She looked playfully surprised to see me take the lead and show off what I could do. It wasn't a back-flip, and I didn't think I'd win a dance competition, but if I could win her heart, that would be just as meaningful.

"Okay! There you go!" she cheered.

At this point, I'm ready to fake it till I make it, and so far, it's working. I spun her again, this time with more confidence and assertiveness. I grinned, happy with how much I've improved in the short time we've been dancing together. But after this spin, she was different. This was a side of Jessica I hadn't seen before.

Jessica closed the gap between us even more, but this time she didn't just close it—she erased it. She stepped closer, wrapped her arms around my neck, and touched her forehead to mine. She kept dancing and swaying perfectly in time with the music. Her warm breath brushed against my lips and nose, carrying the gentle scent of passion fruit sangria from earlier in the night. It wasn't overpowering, just sweet and subtle, much like her. She was simply captivating.

"Yeah, that's my boy D'Angelo!" I heard someone shout. The voice sounded like Ricky in the distance.

Cheerful voices started to break my focus. As much as I wanted to keep gazing into her hazel eyes, the sounds from outside drew my attention. I turned my head just enough to see past Jessica. I noticed some people had stopped dancing and were now watching us—watching me! Some of their faces were familiar from class, and others were from when I first arrived at the party.

Yet, something about the dance floor felt...off.

A sense of death and danger lurked in the corners of the room, hiding behind the smiling faces of the onlookers. It was watching us—watching all of us. I could feel the cosmic shift in the air, the planets had aligned, and the dominoes were already set to fall one by one.

This wasn't just a wave of anxiety. It was a sign. A message.

I took a deep breath and shook off the sudden hysteria pulsing through me, grounding myself as Jessica swayed in my arms.

"Oh boy," I whispered. "It's okay," Jessica said softly. With those two words, she pulled me back from the edge and helped me regain my focus. I went back to dancing with her as we had been.

Looking back, I realized I wasn't just dancing or trying to impress her; I was simply enjoying the moment, stepping out of my comfort zone.

I heard the only English lyrics in the song. This part of the song warned me that it was nearing the end, and it was time to start wrapping things up. I needed to think fast. What could be the perfect way to end this? The crowd began singing along. I dug deep into my mental toolbox for a fitting finale. I eventually found something that might be a bit risky, but why not go for it?

This time, Jessica and I sang the lyrics together. For my final move, I leaned Jessica back and dipped her slightly. I went far enough to make the dip but not so far that I'd risk dropping her or losing my balance. Was it a bit cheesy? Probably. Was it a bit much? Maybe. But in the end, her laughter made it all worthwhile. That was all I needed—it could have gone much worse.

Some people clapped and cheered as we swayed back and found our footing. When the music switched to a song I didn't recognize, the crowd dispersed and went on with their night. All except for Ricky, the man of the hour.

Ricky emerged from the crowd and stood next to Jessica. "That's my bro! That's what I'm talking about!" he said, playfully embarrassing me. He then turned to Jessica. "Did I ever tell you that this guy saved my cat from a burning building?"

"Oh my god," I said with a laugh.

Jessica found it hilarious and threw her head back in laughter. I appreciated Ricky's effort to be my wingman. Everyone could use a friend like him.

I felt a small vibration in my jeans pocket and pulled out my phone. It was a text from Milly saying "911." For us, "911" was a quick way to signal an emergency and that we needed help right away. I remembered Milly had gone out for some air by herself, and my mind immediately jumped to the worst. I couldn't afford to panic; Milly needed me, and it had to be important.

"He can do your taxes! He helps my grandmother cross the street every Sunday when she goes to church!" Ricky continued.

I had to cut him off and make a quick exit.

"Hey, I gotta go. I'll be right back!" I said.

Without another thought, I turned and jogged toward the exit. Jessica's concerned face flashed in my mind, but I knew I had to be there for Milly.

Chapter
TWO

FIVE OF WANDS

I hurried up the small exterior steps to the apartment building, feeling refreshed by the clean, open air outside. The sidewalk was dotted with partygoers, bathed in the glow of the amber streetlights.

I glanced to my left but saw nothing. Then I heard Milly's voice rising above the murmurs of the crowd and the city noise behind me. I turned instantly and saw her standing in front of two people. Without a second thought, I made my way over to her.

I wove through the crowd like it was an obstacle course, dipping and dodging, squeezing past groups of people. Once I made it through, I jogged up beside Milly, unsure of what was going on.

"Hey Milly, what's up? What's the problem?" I asked, a bit out of breath, not paying much attention to the two men standing in front of her.

"These two dickheads won't take no for an answer!" she shouted.

Now that I was up to speed, I turned my attention to the two men facing Milly.

One man had a moderate-sized curly afro, and the other had a short Caesar cut. They both looked to be around my age, maybe a year or two older, like Milly. The man with the afro spoke up.

"Whoa, 'dickheads'?! All I'm saying is, you can come have fun with us!" he said loudly.

"And I've said 'no' several times. Have fun with each other!" Milly shot back.

Some of the other partygoers overheard Milly's comment and laughed. The man with the afro didn't find it amusing and locked eyes with her. His companion glanced over his shoulder, trying to hide a smile. Despite the humor in Milly's remark, I could feel the tension building, and things could easily get out of hand.

"Alright, Milly, I think we should just leave. Don't worry about them." I stepped between them, turning my back on the two men.

"Who's this? Is he your man?" he asked.

"Maybe!" Milly replied with a straight face.

I felt it was only fair to back up Milly's response. I knew I wasn't her "man," though I'd actually love to be, but that wasn't the point.

"Yeah, maybe!" I added, letting a pleased smile show.

"Why don't you mind your own business?" he demanded.

For some reason, his words really got under my skin and sparked a deep anger in me. I snapped around, speaking from my gut rather than my chest.

"She is my business!" I said with my chest, taking a step forward.

Milly started pulling me back. "No, no, no," she pleaded.

Her voice did help me calm down a bit, but I knew I couldn't let my guard down just yet. Fortunately, I didn't, because my heart dropped when I saw the guy with the afro reach into his right back pocket as if he was going to pull out a weapon or something. Everything went silent.

A familiar voice cut through the crowd behind me.

"Yuuurr, what's going on?" I heard.

I turned around and saw Ricky pushing through the crowd, with Jessica right behind him. I'd never been so relieved to see him.

"These guys were harassing Milly," I said.

"Nobody is harassing anybody," the man with the afro protested.

Ricky looked more annoyed than angry or concerned about the situation. I didn't want to cause trouble, especially at Ricky's birthday celebration. He looked down and let out a deep sigh, breaking the silence.

"Joshua, get back inside. Come on," Ricky said firmly.

I shifted my focus back to Joshua, the man with the afro. I watched him and the crowd, waiting to see what he'd do next. Joshua rolled his eyes and started to walk past me and Milly, with his partner following.

"Fucking bitch," Joshua muttered under his breath.

"Yeah, well, fuck you too!" Milly shot back, causing some people to laugh again.

Ricky stayed where he was, giving Joshua a disappointed look as he walked by. From Ricky's expression, it seemed like Joshua had been a problem before.

I noticed Jessica watching from a short distance, her face showing concern. She stood at the edge of the small crowd, her arms folded and shivering slightly from the cold night air.

I felt a bit disappointed in myself, though I knew I shouldn't. I didn't like being the center of negative attention. At least the situation hadn't escalated further.

Milly and I walked over to Ricky, who greeted us with a big smile. Without hesitation, I started to apologize.

"Hey Ricky, I'm sorry for all that—"

He cut me off before I could finish.

"Nah, don't worry about it. Joshua's just a troublemaker. You can't pick your primos," Ricky said with a chuckle.

"Happy birthday again!" Milly said.

I watched as Ricky thanked her and gave her a big hug. Deciding I'd had enough for the night, I figured it was best to head home before it got too late. I had class the next day. But before leaving, there was one more person I needed to say goodbye to.

I walked down the block with Milly and approached Jessica, who seemed to be waiting for me, or maybe just trying to warm up from the cold night air. The macho side of me was nowhere to be found as I greeted her.

"Hey, D'Angelo," she said with concern. "Is everything okay?"

"Yeah, just a couple of assholes," I explained.

I could feel Milly's eyes directed to the side of my head, waiting to see if I would introduce her. Deep down, a part of me did not want these two worlds to collide. I caved in and quickly gestured my hands over to Milly who stood beside me. "This is, um—"

"Milly! Nice to meet you!" Milly cut in.

"Likewise," Jessica replied.

After they shook hands, both of them looked at me with expectant smiles, as if waiting for me to say something next. That was all I needed to end the awkward moment. I had nothing to be ashamed of or to hide, but I usually kept other girls away from Milly because I wasn't sure how they'd react to having a female best friend, or if they'd assume she was my girlfriend. Playing it cool was my way of avoiding unnecessary explanations.

I gave Jessica a hug and told her I'd see her around. As we walked away, Milly kept a smile on her face, probably holding back her thoughts about me and Jessica.

As we strolled down the street, I heard Ricky calling out to me.

"Best in the World!"

Ricky was something special, and looking back, I regretted the trouble Milly and I had caused him. It's wild to
think how one simple decision can dramatically change your
future.

Chapter

THREE

THE FOOL

The Hunts Point Train Station was a large, outdated underground tunnel in desperate need of renovation. The night was still relatively young, which explained why the station was so empty—everyone was either still out partying or already home from work.

As I stood on the platform, I stared down at the tracks below, watching rats scurry along the rails. I was still in a daze, replaying the moment I confronted Joshua for bothering Milly. Behind me, Milly was playfully swinging her arms and walking in circles with her head tilted up, lost in her own world. I turned to my left to observe her in her natural state of wonder and freedom. She glanced over, sensing my gaze, and greeted me with a smile, which I returned.

We boarded the train together. Besides a few people sitting at the far end of the car, it was mostly empty. Milly sat to my left and rested her head on my shoulder.

"Well, that didn't go as planned," she sighed.

"No, but it's okay. I was getting tired anyway, and I have class tomorrow," I replied.

"What?! Tomorrow is Saturday. Who has class on Saturday?"

"Uh, me? I needed the class to get ahead with my credits. Next semester I'll have more free time since I'm taking an extra class now," I explained.

"Oh... still stupid if you ask me," she said.

I burst into laughter. Deep down, I agreed, but I knew it was for the best.

"Thank you for coming to my rescue," she continued.

"No problem, I'll always have your back," I replied.

The forces of the universe must have found that amusing, because it felt like they took it as a challenge.

Milly slowly lifted her head off my shoulder.

"What is that?" she asked.

"What?"

"That, right there."

I followed her gaze to the little white pamphlet stuck in the advertisement frame across from us. All I could make out was a black crystal ball with an eye in the center on the cover. The upper half of the pamphlet was flapping up and down, almost as if it were deliberately trying to catch our attention—waving at us.

Milly stood up and reached for the pamphlet, pulling it out of the frame. She returned to her seat beside me and opened it eagerly. I looked away, uninterested. I had seen these pamphlets plenty of times on my commute and in other places. I always thought they were a scam, or if they weren't, they dealt with things best avoided.

Milly began to read the front of the pamphlet aloud.

"Psychic Medium and Master of the Unknown, 3145 Westchester Avenue! That's not too far from where we live!"

The address rang a bell. It reminded me of a new fortune teller in the neighborhood who'd become well-known over the summer and was dubbed "The Witch of Westchester." I'd heard about her from the neighbors but never realized the pamphlets I'd seen were hers.

"Yeah, I've heard of her," I explained. "She's some kind of witch who does tarot cards or something. Whatever it is, I'm not going to mess with her, and neither should you."

"Aw, come on, don't you want to know your future?" she protested. "I always wanted to do it."

"I already know my future," I joked. "I'm going to graduate college with honors next year, get a puppy—preferably a husky—and name him Milo. And if I play my cards right, I'll have a wife and two kids named Anthony and Angel."

There was some truth to that joke, but I left it for her to figure out. After a light chuckle at my joke, Milly playfully told me to "shut up" and returned to resting her head on my shoulder, though she kept scanning the pamphlet.

My stomach tightened as my intuition warned me that this wasn't the end. When Milly becomes fixated on something—whether it's a boy, a destination, or a trend—she gets almost childlike in her fascination, like a kid with a shiny new toy.

I closed my eyes and rested my head against the train car wall.

IT FELT GOOD TO ACTUALLY HAVE MILLY TAG ALONG to a party belonging to my friend group. Usually, Milly would invite me to go out to parties and sneak into clubs and bars that I was too young to enter into. Those nights were fun—when we didn't get caught ofcourse. Most of the time, when I invited her out there would be some excuse. But I rarely passed up the chance to spend time with her.

We climbed the last set of stairs to my apartment building. A little out of breath, I pulled out my keys, ready to unlock my front door. But just as I was about to do so, the neighboring door across from mine opened. Milly and I paused as we saw Carla, my neighbor, stepping out of her apartment.

Carla was a longtime neighbor who used to hang out with Milly and me in the hallway when we were growing up. She had long flowy hair and was just a bit taller than Milly. Carla was a bit of a townie, more so than Milly, and openly identified as a lesbian, which she made sure Milly and I knew whenever we crossed paths. Seeing Carla, I knew what was coming.

She greeted us with her usual flirtatious smile aimed directly at Milly.

"Hey D'Angelo, Milly," Carla said.

"Hey Carla," I muttered.

"How are you?" Milly asked with amusement.

"I'm good. I'm about to head up to the roof and smoke a blunt—you still have to join me sometime," Carla replied.

"Yeah, I know," Milly said, "but heights kind of freak me out."

"I'm not going to let you fall. Maybe next time."

Even I had to admit that was a pretty good line.

I'm no stranger to being the third wheel with Milly and her love interests, but there was something particularly off-putting about being there when Carla tried to flirt with Milly. You'd think I'd find it kind of hot seeing two girls interact with sexual tension, but not this time. If I remember correctly, Milly and Carla never did anything physical, nor had Milly ever mentioned it. I'm sure Milly enjoyed the attention, though.

"Yeah, maybe next time," Milly said.

Carla kept eye contact with Milly as long as she could before turning and heading up to the rooftop. I almost felt like I was intruding, just standing there.

As Carla disappeared into the dark corner of the staircase, I paused for a moment before breaking the silence.

"What if I wanted to go?" I asked with a grin.

"You don't smoke weed!" Milly replied.

"I know, but it's the thought that counts," I said.

"Boy, open the door!" Milly demanded, clearly done with my jokes.

I unlocked the front door and slowly pushed it open. As I stepped into the foyer, I glanced toward the dark hallway leading to my blind grandmother's bedroom, straining to hear if she was awake. Not hearing anything, I signaled for Milly to follow me quietly down the opposite direction to my bedroom. She gently closed the door behind us.

I opened my bedroom door, revealing a space that still had a childlike charm in its decor. Lego Bionicles lined the shelves above my twin bed. Opposite the bed was my Apple computer and desk, cluttered with books, papers, pens, and sticky notes. A 27-inch flat-screen TV was mounted on the wall between the computer and the bed. The room was surrounded by white and baby blue walls.

Milly and I walked in, enjoying the cozy atmosphere. As I sat on the edge of my bed, Milly's attention was drawn to the large tapestry hanging on the back wall.

"Aw, nice tapestry!" Milly said.

It was the tapestry Milly had given me before she moved out to live with her sister years ago, depicting a mystical tree and forest. I finally hung it up a few months back.

"Thanks, a friend gave it to me," I said. "By the way, I have to give credit to Carla—she's pretty persistent. Reminds me of how I was with you when we were younger. Would you ever...?"

"Maybe, I don't know," she said, her gaze dropping as she fidgeted with her nails. She walked over and sat beside me on the edge of my bed. "But what about you and that girl- Jessica? I saw the way you were looking at her."

I felt like I was in an interrogation room when she asked me that. I don't know why, but it felt like I was being caught cheating. My loyalty sometimes felt utterly delusional. I had to play it cool.

"Oh, that was nothing," I said. "I highly doubt I'd even have a chance with her, even if I tried."

"You could," she said softly. "She'd be lucky to have you. Why don't you read her some of your poetry?"

I was living in a world where one girl, whom I used to write poetry for, was now telling me to write poetry for another girl. Her suggestion left me confused, making me want to respond in a dozen different ways. I considered mentioning the past and how I used to have feelings for her when we were kids, or maybe reminding her of something I once wrote for her. But all I could manage was a bewildered look. Before I could say anything, she laughed to herself, broke eye contact, and stood up.

"It's hot in here. Hold on, I'm going to open a window, if that's okay."

"Yeah, of course. Go ahead."

It might have been the alcohol making us feel overheated, or maybe it was just the moment I was sharing with Milly that was making me feel so warm.

I watched her open the window next to my computer desk. After she opened it, she crouched down and rested her arms against the windowsill, letting the fresh night air brush against her face. I admired how carefree she was.

Seeing her admiring the night air peacefully in the moment reminded me of the lively and easygoing spirit she had.

Like a caged bird, she craved adventure and flowing with the wind, yet she was stuck in The Bronx, reduced to only using her imagination of venturing out in the world even if that would be in the middle of nowhere. Maybe anything would've been better than staying here in the city.

She wasn't the only one who wanted to move out of The Bronx, I'm sure most people did, including myself. Unlike her, and maybe a lot of other people, I on the other hand had a little bit more of a meticulous plan of bettering myself and doing what it took to move out and into one of the better neighborhoods. I was banking on a college education, becoming financially literate, having multiple streams of income and more.

My gaze wandered down and I noticed her rear. I couldn't help it; it was right there. Milly stood up straight and glanced back at me, squinting as if she knew I was looking. I shrugged and gave her a confused look. All she did was smirk.

"Okay, what time is it?" she asked, as if changing the subject.

I glanced at the cable box beside her. "It's 10 o'clock," I replied.

"Hm, the night is still young," she said, tapping her chin with a grin.

I rolled my eyes, knowing this meant Milly was about to suggest something I probably wouldn't want to do. "Oh man, what is it?" I asked.

"Listen, hear me out. How about we go to the fortune teller while we still have time?" she proposed.

I couldn't hide my disapproval and annoyance as I was surprised she was still on this topic. I had to correct her.

"First of all, you mean the Witch of Westchester. And I thought I already said we shouldn't mess around with that."

"D, please, live a little! We can go, and she can do a reading just for me!"

"It's 10 o'clock. She should be closed by now," I explained.

Without hesitation, Milly pulled the pamphlet from her back pocket.

"No! It says here she's open from 5 PM to 1 AM," she said, holding the pamphlet out to me.

I looked at the pamphlet between us with a look of drained disappointment. I was frustrated that the hours of operation weren't a big enough red flag for Milly. But leave it to her to see red flags as an amusement park. I glanced up past the pamphlet and saw Milly's wide, pleading eyes, begging me to give in.

"Please, just for me," she urged.

I had to stand my ground. I sat up, looked Milly dead in the eye, and spoke with conviction.

"Milly, let me be perfectly clear. There is no way in hell I'm going to that place!"

Chapter
FOUR

THE DEVIL

I'm not sure how it happened, but before I knew it, Milly was dragging me by the arm up Westchester Ave, heading toward the witch's house.

The streetlamp's light was blocked by the dense trees lining the sidewalk, making it nearly impossible to see. A steady gust of wind pushed against us, as if trying to turn us back. But that didn't deter Milly; she was determined to reach her destination.

The eerie environment and sense of impending doom made it hard for me to breathe. I kept scanning the shadows, half-expecting someone to be lurking and waiting for the right moment to rob or kill us.

How could someone I care about so much be willing to put me in danger? She was the devil on my shoulder, and I was the angel on hers. I don't think Milly ever intended to hurt me; she was driven by the thrill of her actions, and sometimes those actions led to self-destruction. It wasn't until I put out the flames that she might truly grasp the seriousness of her actions and choices. These weren't random mistakes but rather a part of her nature. Maybe she even took some strange satisfaction in challenging my innocence. Over the years, I held a slight hope that I could influence her for the better, but who was I to try to tame a devil?

"Come on! We're almost there. Stop being such a baby," she snapped.

"You know, if you get possessed by some negative spirit, I'm not helping you," I warned.

"Oh really? It's not that bad. Look, we're here!" she said.

We paused. I took in the sight of the old, weathered house nestled between two large London Plane trees, bathed in a pool of amber streetlight. The house looked poorly maintained, with dead leaves strewn across the small front porch and paint peeling from the wooden door. The short black iron gate, reaching our hips, stood unlocked and gently swayed in the wind. I noticed no light coming from the windows, and there was no sign of movement inside. After a moment of tense silence, I decided to break it.

"Okay, well I don't think anyone's home. Let's go," I said, sharply turning away.

Milly grabbed my leather jacket sleeve, pulling me back beside her.

"Hold on," she said with a dragging tone. "We haven't knocked yet."

As she pushed open the old gate, the situation suddenly felt all too real and overwhelming. Part of me hoped Milly would reconsider now that we were in front of the house, but of course, she didn't.

Slowly and steadily, Milly approached the front door, as if she were walking to the edge of a diving board, ready to plunge into the unknown. With each step, the air in my lungs felt denser, as if I were the one sinking into the cold unforgiving darkness.

She climbed the small staircase to the stoop and gave a weak knock on the door.

A moment passed. I looked up the sidewalk to take a breath; it was the only way to calm my nerves. I couldn't shake the feeling that someone was watching us. She knocked again, this time with a bit more assertiveness.

"Hello, is anyone there?" Milly called out.

"Milly, I don't think she's home."

"Wait," she said, glancing over her shoulder.

Milly knocked three more times.

One. Two. Three.

The air grew still, and everything seemed quieter than usual. This was our last chance to leave. In uncomfortable situations, I do what I do best—bring humor into the mix. It's a coping mechanism, or some might call it a superpower.

"Milly, I'm going to be honest with you. I'm Black, so in horror movies, things usually don't end well for guys like me."

Milly lowered her head, maybe to hide her laughter or maybe out of defeat.

"So, I'm going," I continued.

"It's whatever. I don't think anyone's here," she sighed, turning to face me.

The lump in my throat eased as I felt a wave of relief, knowing I'd live to see another day. I turned and was over-joyed to hear Milly's footsteps coming down the stoop be-hind me. The sound of victory was soon disrupted and over-shadowed by a new, unsettling noise.

The sound of an eerie creak sent shockwaves through my spine, stopping me in my tracks. I hesitated to turn around, but curiosity got the better of me. When I finally did, I saw an image that would haunt me for the rest of my life.

An elderly woman with a red headscarf peeked out from the doorway. Her high cheekbones and wrinkled forehead were striking, but nothing compared to her dark, piercing eyes that locked onto me in the darkness, making me feel like a fly caught in her web. A large, devilish smile emerged from the shadows of her face.

"Come in, children. How may I be of service to you?" she said.

"Oh, come on," I muttered to myself.

She held the door open with a welcoming gesture, wav-ing us inside as if she knew exactly why we were there.

Milly stepped toward the elderly lady with keen interest. I watched Milly walk into the abyss, and my legs followed along as if they had a mind of their own, ready to pounce and save Milly from falling.

"Are you the Fortune Teller?" Milly asked.

Who else could she be? I thought.

The elderly lady bowed her head, her smile unwavering, and her arm still extended, inviting us inside.

"At your service, dear," she replied.

Milly moved toward the front door and looked back at me, waiting for me to join. Behind her, the Fortune Teller's gaze locked onto me, her devious smile seeming to acknowledge that she had me in her grasp now that Milly was already inside. With my resolve crumbling, I followed Milly into the house.

We were now in the witch's den. Candles lit up both ends of the narrow foyer. One candle, near the front door, sat on a small, dusty table next to a murky black-and-white photo and an old book. The floor creaked beneath us.

"I am Madame Maria Mejia—Madame Maria for short," she said as she closed the door. "Master of the Unknown. I've been expecting two wandering souls today."

If that was the case, you'd think she'd tidy up the place or answer the door a bit sooner, but to each their own.

Madame Maria started to walk past us, down the narrow foyer.

"Milly, are you sure about this?" I asked in a hushed whisper.

She shushed me urgently.

"Come to my Enchanting Room," Madame Maria said, waving for us to follow.

Milly followed with wide, innocent eyes, as if all her dreams were about to come true. I trailed behind her, on high alert and bracing for the worst. At the end of the foyer, we turned left into a spacious living room cluttered with oddities and curiosities. Leather-bound books lined the shelves of a large wooden bookcase behind a wooden desk, where thick red candles burned at each end. On the desk, a collection of pamphlets, books, and newspapers lay coated in dust.

We stepped into the living room briefly and turned to the right, through an open door that led to the Enchanting Room.

The Enchanting Room felt different as soon as we stepped past the door frame. It was damp and cold, as if we had entered a dungeon with a heavy draft, though there were no windows. An invisible vortex seemed to swirl around the room, stirring my emotions and giving me a queasy feeling, making me wonder what the heck we had just walked into.

Against a partially exposed brick wall stood a table with two chairs on one side and a single chair on the other. A long white candle and a deck of tarot cards rested on the table. Behind the lone chair, a large black tapestry adorned with moon phases hung against the wall. Aside from the table setup, the room was spacious and empty.

Madame Maria moved briskly toward the table.

"Come, come, please take a seat, children. No need to be scared!" she proclaimed.

I had every reason to be afraid, and I was twice her size and possibly a fourth of her age.

Milly and I approached the chairs, the wooden floor creaking beneath our feet. As we sat down, I thought it might help to engage in conversation to break the ice and ease the tension in the room.

"So you said you were expecting us? How is that?"

"Well, I sensed a passionate couple in need of my guidance. There is a lot of fear and anger within you—"

The words *"passionate couple"* echoed in my mind. Milly and I exchanged a quick glance, both of us registering the same alarm.

"—especially after the encounter with the stubborn bull today. You two want many things, but I can only do so much in one sitting."

Despite my skeptical mindset, Madame Maria managed to pique my interest, just a little. The gears in my head started to turn, and I felt a pull to engage more in the conversation. But my instincts reminded me that this woman was a master at what she did, whether that was scamming people or actually dabbling in dark arts. Either way, I needed to stay steady, headstrong, and vigilant. Someone had to, especially since Milly seemed ready to dive headfirst into this.

"Oh no, this isn't for me; it's for her," I said, pointing at Milly.

Milly gave a coy smile.

Madame Maria fixed me with a deep, knowing gaze, accompanied by an innocent smile. It was the kind of look a grandmother gives when she already knows the answer because of her wisdom. It reminded me of the look my own grandmother used to give me before she lost her sight a few years ago.

"Oh, I know my pure-hearted child, but relax. Nothing bad will happen to you! Just some simple tarot cards, maybe a hand reading, or perhaps some elderly advice. No black magic," she assured. "But if you prefer, D'Angelo, you can wait in the next room. I will take good care of her!"

I glanced back at Milly, eager to take the invitation and escape. It seemed like a good idea to me. I gave her a pat on the back before leaving the table.

"Well, you don't have to tell me twice," I joked. "Good luck with all this."

I walked to the door, relieved to be cut loose from this web and finally able to breathe a bit more easily. As I reached for the doorknob, ready to make my escape, I froze. The blood drained from my face, and my mouth went dry. I turned my head sharply and asked, "Wait a minute—"

"Wait, did she just say my name? How do you know my name?"

"Angelo, please, it's almost closing time!" Madame Maria snapped with an accent.

Her commanding tone jolted me out of my trance. In my fear and adrenaline, I accidentally walked into the door I was about to open. I regained my composure and yanked the doorknob open. As I glanced back before closing the door, I saw Milly and Madame Maria sharing a chuckle over my frantic, clumsy exit. Despite my amazement at how she knew my name, I remained on edge, wary of who or what Madame Maria truly was.

"He is a good boy."

"Yeah, he's my best friend," Milly responded.

Those were the last words I heard before closing the door completely. They brought me a small wave of comfort, reminding me why I was there in the first place and reassuring me that Milly valued me. It was also a relief to know that Madame Maria, whether a magic sorceress or a scam artist, saw me in a positive light.

Away from the chaotic vortex of emotions in the other room, I finally had a chance to breathe in a new environment. The living room was dusty and dimly lit, which didn't do much to ease my anxiety. I tried to focus on positive thoughts.

This is a cool experience, look at all these interesting knick-knacks, books, and treasures—oh my god, is that a human skull?

I leaned in toward the middle shelf of the bookcase for a closer look at the skull. I'd seen decorative skulls before, but this one looked disturbingly realistic. Given Madame Maria's profession, the skull added an unsettling touch of authenticity.

The empty eye sockets were particularly unsettling. I felt uneasy looking into those dark holes, almost as if I were impolitely staring at someone's private moment. When I found the skull hidden between two bookends, it made me feel a bit sad. I was raised to think that human remains should be buried to let the dead rest peacefully, not displayed as decoration in a witch's lair.

If only it could speak, I wonder what it would say. How did it end up here? Whose head was it? What's the story behind everything in this house?

With my curiosity piqued, I grew concerned about what might be hiding in the shadows of this house. I took out my cell phone, turned on its flashlight, and nervously glanced around to ensure nothing dangerous was lurking in the dark. The dust sparkling in the beam of light made it seem like I was in the middle of a snowstorm, which might explain the difficulty I had breathing.

I focused again on the bookshelf and noticed a row of books with faded spines and some that weren't even in English. In the empty spaces, there were trinkets and odd items like crystals, porcelain dolls, and a variety of vials containing tiny bones, feathers, and insects. Cobwebs connected them all together.

Feeling like I was about to be caught trespassing, I glanced back at the door leading to the enchanting room, bracing myself for it to swing open. After a few tense moments, I realized it was okay to continue exploring the room and its secrets.

To my left, a large wooden desk stood between me and the door to the enchanting room. With my cell phone's light guiding me, I tiptoed my way to the cluttered desk. My attention was drawn to a small mountain of pamphlets and newspapers piled between two burning red candles.

I glanced over the stack of printed papers on the desk, scanning the cover pages that were legible. I felt a pull toward them, as they seemed like the safest thing to touch, helping me ground myself and satisfy my curiosity.

As I looked from side to side across the sea of white and black headlines, one gray, dusty newspaper caught my eye.

It stuck out from the bottom of the pile, the word *"Dead"* glaring at me as if it were pleading for attention, buried beneath the heap.

Without much thought, my hand reached out for the newspaper. As I glided past the candle, I was inches away from grabbing its edge when a stern voice barked from beyond the door to the Enchanting Room. I snatched my hand back, afraid of getting caught red-handed.

I couldn't make out what was said, but it definitely wasn't Milly—her voice was never that harsh. I was tempted to burst through the door and ask what was going on, but the house fell silent immediately after, as if nothing had happened at all.

The interruption reminded me that my time alone in the living room was limited, so I needed to act quickly to satisfy my curiosity.

I refocused on the desk and with a steadier hand, carefully pulled out the edge of the newspaper just enough to read the headline. Tilting my head to get a better look, I saw it read: *"High School Football Star Found Dead."* The headline struck me as particularly odd because I hadn't heard of any such incident.

After successfully uncovering the first newspaper, it became easier to push my boundaries. Without much thought, I shifted the pile of papers aside, revealing another newspaper covered in what looked like satanic symbols scribbled in red ink.

A wave of danger washed over me, and I felt tiny needles of fear prickling from my palms to my fingertips. I knew I had to act fast—it was time to leave.

I marched over to the closed door leading to the Enchanting Room and swung it open with authority. But nothing could have prepared me for what I saw on the other side.

Milly was pressed against the wall in the center of a red pentagram where the tapestry had been moments before. Her head hung low, as if she was too exhausted to notice my sudden entrance.

Madam Maria stood in front of Milly with one arm raised, looking back over her shoulder as if she was caught red-handed, clearly surprised by my sudden entrance.

I scanned the room, trying to make sense of the scene. A tarot card reading was spread out on the table, the tapestry lay on the floor, and Milly's feet were hovering a foot off the ground.

I couldn't understand how such an extreme situation could unfold in just a matter of minutes.

"What the hell are you doing?" I cried out.

"D'Angelo, stay right there!" Madame Maria warned.

My attention was drawn to movement above Madame Maria. Milly slowly turned her head to face me. As she opened her eyes, a white light began to radiate outward. Then, Milly's eyes shot wide open.

"D'Angelo?" she asked. "Wha—what's happening?"

I looked up in agony, seeing Milly so helpless. The endless void within her glowing white eye sockets terrified me to my core. I could do nothing but watch in horror.

Milly's head swiveled back and forth in confusion, scanning the room. She glanced at her wrists, pressed tightly against the wall high at her sides. She clenched her fists and tried to pull her arms free, as if they were bound by chains.

"Milly, do not fight it!" Madam Maria called out.

"I wanna go home!" Milly wept.

Milly yanked her arms up and down, desperately trying to break free from her invisible restraints. With a sudden burst of energy, she managed to pull her wrists off the wall and move her arms freely.

The floor beneath my feet started to shake, accompanied by the sound of a woman screeching, though no one was visible.

Madam Maria screamed at the top of her lungs, pleading with Milly. "Milly, you have to let me finish!"

Her words only made things worse. Milly began clawing at her waist, desperately trying to free herself from the last restraint holding her against the pentagram. Her frustration had turned to rage.

"Meri—I order you to stop!" Madam Maria shouted.

Milly froze in place, her head hung low as she took rapid, deep breaths. Her red curls draped over her eyes. In an instant, she snapped her head up and snarled at Madam Maria with intense anger. Small black veins covered the side of her face. She began thrashing wildly, like a rabid animal, pounding her hands and feet furiously against the wall.

I knew I didn't want to be there when Milly got off that wall, certain that what stood before me was no longer Milly.

My eyes and heart wanted to reach out and yank her off the wall, but my brain and gut were pleading with me to run the other way as this was beyond my help.

I turned and bolted out of the room, racing into the darkness of Madam Maria's house. I wasn't afraid of the dark anymore; I was only terrified of what had become of Milly.

A deep, raspy voice called out from behind me, "D'Angelo!" It sounded like Milly but was much deeper and more menacing.

I threw open the front door and found myself in a thunderstorm. There was no time to worry about getting soaked as the pounding footsteps behind me grew louder and closer. I lunged off the small stoop, sharply turning past the miniature iron gate. My only focus was getting home and surviving the night.

Chapter
FIVE

SIX OF SWORDS

I ran down the dark street of Westchester Ave. The sidewalk that had been so easy to walk earlier was now a treacherous obstacle course. I ducked and dodged low-hanging branches and trash cans, jumped over cracked pavement, all while drenched in rain.

There was no one in sight, but I knew I wasn't alone—I was being hunted. Deep grunts and heavy footsteps followed me, crashing through the trash cans and branches I had avoided. I couldn't look back—I was too terrified.

I turned the corner, escaping the darkness of Westchester Ave. I finally reached the bright light of the supermarket that stretched nearly the entire block, but I knew I wasn't safe yet. The brightness only made me run faster as I could now see clearly.

I made a sharp left at the corner and crossed the street diagonally, narrowly avoiding a car that almost hit me just a hundred feet from my apartment building. I thanked God the car stopped in time.

Breathless, I fumbled to get my keys out of my jacket pocket. A few feet from the front door, I could see into my building's lobby through the glass window. Just as I was almost at the finish line, my keys slipped from my grasp and fell onto the wet pavement.

In a moment of panic, I instinctively crouched and looked behind me, fearing that I had lost this game of cat and mouse. I thought this might be the end of the chase—and the end of me. I scanned the area, expecting something to appear from behind a car or emerge from the dense rainfall. I strained to hear past the rain and my own labored breathing. Everything seemed normal, but I wasn't about to let my guard down.

I snatched my keys off the wet ground, shoved the front door key into the keyhole, and burst inside. I slammed the heavy door behind me and fell backward, gasping for air.

Once inside my apartment, I shut the door behind me and engaged all three locks.

Finally, safe within the warmth of my own home, I leaned against the door, catching my breath. I stared into the dark hallway leading to my grandma's room, trying to make sense of it all.

What just happened? What was Milly doing? What was chasing me? Nothing made sense, and I couldn't find a logical explanation for anything I had just witnessed.

I couldn't stay still for long; I was still in fight-or-flight mode. I stood up straight, took a deep breath, and marched to my room, eager for some refuge. But as soon as I opened the door, the sound of rain hit me, bringing with it a fresh wave of fear and anxiety.

Milly had left the bedroom window open earlier, and it was still wide open. Heavy rain droplets were splattering on the windowsill, creating a small puddle on the floor. A flash of lightning cut through the darkness, jolting me from my daze.

I approached the open window with great caution, bracing myself for whatever might be on the other side. I raised my hands slightly and continued forward, preparing to close the window.

The distant rumble of thunder echoed around me, and the sound of rain crashing against the windowsill grew louder.

I took a deep breath, grasped the edge of the window firmly, and shut it with determination. I paused for a moment, bracing myself for something to appear on the other side of the closed window, but there was nothing. I sighed with relief and relaxed my arms, but I remained tense. I took a few steps back, still keeping the window in sight, unwilling to let my guard down.

The hairs on the back of my neck stood up as a chill ran down my spine. My instincts kicked in, making me feel like prey about to be pounced on by a bloodthirsty wolf. But there was no time for instincts; I would already be dead.

Suddenly, I felt hands caressing my stomach and chest from behind, and a light weight pressed against my upper back. Startled, I let out a small scream. I turned around, expecting to be devoured by a demonic and ravenous version of Milly but it was just her with melancholic eyes. She took a step back, snatching her hands back down to her sides, as if my reaction startled her.

Her embrace might have been brief, but I could still feel the warm and comforting embrace of her arms wrapped around me. I was confused and asked myself; did she just hug me?

Milly stood there, soaking wet, with pitiful eyes fixed on me like a child coming to a parent after a misstep. Her eyes were glistening with tears, and her shoulders were covered in grime, as if she had just finished sweeping a chimney.

"Milly?" I exclaimed. "What the hell did you do?"

"I don't know," she muttered.

I pressed on with my questions. "How did you beat me here? What happened in that room?"

"I don't know!" she shouted.

I clenched my fists and took a firm stance, glaring deeply into her doe-like eyes. I wasn't even sure if she was the one chasing me anymore as nothing was making sense. "What was chasing me?" I asked firmly, pointing at the window.

She took a moment to glance past my shoulder at the window, then returned her gaze to me with a sharp look.

"Something was chasing you?" Milly responded.

At that moment, I realized she was just as confused as I was.

The sound of shuffling footsteps outside my bedroom door barely registered as I focused on Milly, until I heard a light, calming, and familiar voice.

"D'Angelo? Who are you talking to?" the voice asked.

I looked to my left and saw my blind grandmother standing in the bedroom doorway, wearing her pink pajamas. She looked helpless and lost.

My grandma has been blind for a few years now due to cataracts, but that hasn't stopped her from moving about the house and handling most of her daily activities. As long as the house is clean and nothing is too out of place, she can still navigate and find whatever she needs. She knows Milly well and sees her almost like a granddaughter, accepting her as part of the family.

I had to think quickly.

"Um, hi Grandma," I muttered. "I was just on the phone."

"Oh, I thought I heard Milly," she said.

"Oh, you probably did, but—she's asleep right now," I stammered.

"Hey, why didn't the two of you ever get together?" she whispered.

The question made Milly grin and widen her eyes. The tension in the room was palpable, and she looked at me, waiting for my response.

"Oh, you know Milly," I said with a chuckle. "She has bad taste in men—guess I'm just not her cup of tea."

Milly glanced at me and punched my shoulder—not her usual playful tap, but a forceful hit, like a man's punch. I even heard a faint, ghostly hiss when she made contact. Trying to maintain the illusion that I was alone in the room, I swallowed my pain and kept silent.

My grandma gave another innocent smile, accepted the answer, and turned to leave.

Still wincing, I turned away and began to rub my shoulder. Just when I thought I would hear her footsteps fade away, my grandma stayed and asked another question.

"What's that smell? Is something burning?" she asked with concern.

Milly looked increasingly nervous, as if she were being cornered.

"Barbecue!" I blurted out, trying to mask my pain and frustration. "They were barbecuing outside, so I shut the window."

I soon realized that the burnt smell was coming from Milly. She must have picked it up from the cookout at the gates of hell, apparently.

I knew I had to end this conversation as soon as possible, or my Grandma would start a whole new discussion. My grandma loved to talk but now was not the time. I walked toward her, guiding her out of my room.

"Yeah, Grandma," I said, trying to sound as natural as possible. "I had a long day and I'm about to go to sleep." I gently placed my hands on her shoulders and turned her toward the door. She felt along the door frame to orient herself. "So, have a good night. I love you, and watch your step," I added.

Why did I say that last part?

"I love you too. Use a condom!" she said as I closed the door behind her.

I pressed my weight against the bedroom door and turned to face Milly, anxious about her reaction to everything that had happened with my Grandma. Instead of laughing or showing any other emotion, she stood in the middle of my room, looking drained and exhausted. After everything that had happened in the last few hours, I was ready to call it a night.

"Okay, Milly, it's been a long day. I think it's best if we meet tomorrow—"

"I'm tired," she cut me off.

I paused in confusion as I watched her move toward my bed.

"Yeah, okay, I get it. I'm tired too, but I think you should go home and—"

Before I could finish, she collapsed onto my bed and made herself comfortable. I didn't know whether to be more disturbed or fascinated: she was in my bed—fully clothed, soaking wet, and dirty. Or was it more surprising that, after everything that had happened, she could fall asleep within seconds?

Feeling defeated, I threw up my hands and let them slap against my thighs before quietly leaving the room.

Later, I returned to my room, now wearing a fresh white T-shirt and checkered pajama pants. I carefully closed the door behind me and turned my attention to Milly, who was deeply asleep in my bed.

I wasn't thrilled about sharing a room with someone who had just come back from a ritual with a witch, but I couldn't help but feel sorry for Milly. She's been a part of my life for a long time, and despite everything, I still care a great deal about her.

I bent down and carefully took off Milly's sneakers, gently placing them on the floor. I reached over and grabbed an extra pillow from beside her and set it down on the blue shaggy rug next to my twin bed.

I sat down and lay back, resting my head on the pillow. As I stared at the ceiling, I replayed the night's chaotic moments in my mind. I had gone from being inches away from Jessica's lips to inches away from death—quite a leap for one night, if you ask me. Despite feeling overwhelmed and confused about what had happened, a sense of pride began to seep into me.

The feeling of victory, surviving a death-defying adventure comforted me and eased me into a deep sleep, which turned out to be a snare trap into a vivid, lucid nightmare. A nightmare that I will never forget.

Chapter

SIX

THE MOON

R ed. The first thing I saw was the color red blanketing my bedroom ceiling. The red light was being projected from the lamp next to my TV.

My eyes twitched around the bedroom ceiling, as that was the only thing I was able to do. I lay there, on my bedroom floor motionless and helpless. My mind desperately tried to send signals to my body to move, but nothing. I couldn't talk; I was barely able to breathe. I was glued to the floor with the sense of impending doom taking over.

Milly! Where's Milly? I thought. *She should still be in my bed.*

I shifted my eyes to the right, hoping to see any sign of life—any sign of hope. I begged for Milly to wake up, to help me.

Milly! Help! Wake up! I begged with my thoughts.

Just as I thought all hope was lost, Milly peered over the edge of my bed eagerly. She looked down at me like I was a little boy trapped at the bottom of a well. With her curly hair tunneling her face, I saw her innocent smile. She could see that my eyes were pleading for help. Instead, she crawled back swiftly, disappearing past the edge of my bed. The sound of her giggle echoed.

NO! Come back! I screamed internally. But she was far from being gone.

She emerged, crawling up from the base of my abdomen. Her eyes examined me, admiring every inch of my body as if I were a delicacy. Raising her head slightly, she met my eyes with a seductive, playful smile. She continued to slither her way up to meet me face to face.

"Hey D'Angelo," she greeted softly. Her words echoed deep in my brain, as if they were soaking into my subconscious.

She cupped the side of my face, brushing my cheek with her thumb. After taking a second to admire my lips, her eyes shot back up to look deep into my own.

"You're so cute when you're sleeping. Have I ever told you that?" she asked.

She rested her head in the center of my chest and straddled me. It was almost as if she was enjoying the sound of my heart beat. Her body weight made it increasingly harder to breathe.

I quickly realized that I must have been dreaming and none of this was real. I shut my eyes hoping it was over. After a moment, I opened them, only to find her standing with one foot on my chest, bending over looking down with her large doe-like eyes, as if she were waiting to watch me slowly die, and for my soul to depart from my body.

I gasped for air and closed my eyes again, wishing this nightmare would come to an end.

I opened them to her straddling me once again, but the weight she pressed against my chest did not lighten one bit.

What do I believe? What is real? I pondered.

Like a dog, she took a deep sniff of my chest, followed by several other smaller sniffs. After exhaling, she dreadfully looked up at me with great concern in her eyes, as if something was wrong.

"You're... different" she said.

For a moment, her lips parted and her eyes danced across my face, as if she were confused. We both were.

I began to hear a flurry of things. Voices that sounded like Milly's whispered in my ear.

"Wake up" a voice demanded. "Run D'Angelo! Run!" Another voice pleaded. Yet

an increasingly loud, angelic tone of voice harmonized in the distance. Although faint, it was still beautiful and somewhat alluring, even in the face of danger.

Gradually Milly's facial expression had changed, becoming hyper focused as if she had her mind set. Sitting up straight on her knees, she leaned back and opened her mouth. Fangs protruded from her gums, snapping out like twigs breaking apart.

At that moment it all made sense to me. I was at her mercy all along, and I couldn't breathe because I was drowning, with Milly being the one anchoring me down. I wasn't just a boy trapped at the bottom of a well, I was a fly trapped in the web of a deadly spider. She had me right where she wanted me.

Milly locked her predatorial eyes onto me one last time.

"Aww" she moaned. "You can't die now D'Angelo, we're just starting to have fun."

Like a viper, she snapped towards me, and like a helpless hare, all I could do was accept my fate. But instead of hearing the sound of holy trumpets at the gates of heaven, I heard the alarm on my phone go off.

Chapter

SEVEN

ACE OF SWORDS — REVERSED

I jerked up from the floor awakened from my nightmare, clawing at my throat in a desperate attempt to catch my breath. I sat there panting in a cold sweat as if I just surfaced from diving in a pool. The white morning sunlight beamed down on my face, although slightly blinding me, it assured me that I was now safe from the clutches of my nightmare. I turned around and shut off the alarm from my phone.

"Milly!" I called out while clearing my throat. "Milly!"

I found her just as she was last night in my bed. She laid there looking so peaceful and graceful like sleeping beauty. She sluggishly turned around, awakening from her own slumber. Dazed and confused, she eventually focused her attention on me.

"Hey, what's up?" she asked.

Wasting no time, I pieced together what I could remember and I shared my nightmare experience, battling through my dry mouth and throat.

"I just had a crazy dream, you- you were trying to kill me!" I said panting. "And I couldn't breathe-." I turned to see the confused and concerned look she was giving me. I looked up at the ceiling to find a moment of clarity, but that only made matters worse and even more strange. I examined my bedroom ceiling in bewilderment.

"What the hell is that?" I asked, causing Milly to turn and match my gaze.

Marked above my door frame were several black foot and claw prints that led up to the ceiling just above my bed where Milly was sleeping.

I laid there on the floor, looking up, terrified at the sight of the claw marks. *What could possibly have done that?* I wondered. No human could have done this.

I turned my attention to Milly in fear as she is the only culprit who I thought could be responsible for this. Milly looked down at me, but not in fear, but instead concern and possibly guilt. I fell back onto my pillow, accepting defeat, staring at the light fixture above me with a blank face.

"What do you think it means?" asked Milly.

"It means we fucked up big time Mills" I said firmly.

"You don't think—"

"Who the hell else could it be Milly?" I asked, snatching myself up from the floor.

"It wasn't me!"

"Okay, let's ask the girl who sacrificed herself last night—oh wait, we're back to you!"

Milly stood up from the bed and faced me with a pitiful look.

"D'Angelo, I didn't sacrifice myself" she assured. "She said it was a protection spell." Her voice remained confident and steady. Her denial over the severity angered me as if I was talking to a brick wall trying to make Milly realize that this was far from a protection spell. With a lack of quality sleep, and making no progress in having Milly taking accountability, I decided to try a new tactic in explaining the gravity of the situation.

"Milly, have I ever called you out of your name?" I asked.

"Uh, no."

"Great, so don't take this personally when I say this—" I figured I'd cushion the blow before I said what I felt needed to be said. "Bitch! You were floating off of a pentagram, and you popped into my room, and I woke up to claw marks on my ceiling!" I paused in fear, wondering how Milly would react to me calling her a 'bitch'. She cracked a grin, then broke out into her iconic laughter.

I stood there momentarily in disbelief. I just explained the dire situation we were in, and called her a bitch, and all she could do was laugh? Although her taking the situation so lightly wasn't so much of a surprise to me, it only infuriated me.

"So you think this is funny?" I passed by her on my way to the bathroom to brush my teeth. I gazed upon the claw marks above my door frame as I exited. I could still hear her chuckling from behind me.

After brushing my teeth and changing into some fresh clothes I returned to my room with Milly sitting on the edge of my bed maintaining a grin on her face.

I yanked my book bag off of the computer chair and placed it on my shoulder. Milly decided to break the awkward silence.

"Look D, it's not funny, maybe a little bit-" she chuckles. "But look just take a mop and scrub it off or something"

"Mills, you're not getting the point. This is something demonic and it's clearly following us and knows we're here. Whatever this is, you did this."

I looked at the time on the cable box. *8:35AM* I read. My biology class that I needed to go to that morning crossed my mind, snapping me out of the conversation.

Her eye contact did not yield.

"Milly I gotta go, but honestly something clearly followed us from last night!"

"What do you want me to do?"

Milly looked at me, with fear in her eyes not just because of the possible repercussions, but maybe because she's not used to seeing me as bothered as I was. To see me actually angry and voicing my frustration over something she caused, probably makes her feel lower than anyone else that scolds her. Maybe she understood this wasn't something we could laugh off.

I took a second to think and digest everything. I had to be strong, I had to think straight or things will only get worse. I grabbed my book bag from my computer chair and placed it on my shoulder.

"Look Milly just do me a favor just don't get into any trouble while I'm gone, okay?"

Fighting tears, Milly nodded.

"Go home and we'll meet up later okay? Everything is gonna be okay and we're gonna get to the bottom of this."

I gave Milly a hug. I'm not sure who needed the hug more honestly, me or her. Usually when we hug it would feel refreshing to me. A hug from her gives me a boost and a breath of fresh air, which is ironic because in my dream she was suffocating the life out of me, but what's even more alarming was that this hug felt different. As we embraced, I tilted my head up to see the markings on the ceiling one last time.

I walked past Milly to exit my bedroom.

"D!" she said, halting me in my tracks. "I really am sorry."

"I know."

LATER I EVENTUALLY MADE IT TO LEHMAN COLLEGE and sat in my biology class, which wasn't one of my favorite classes, but it sounded interesting and I needed an elective for college credits. Extremely tired, I sat in my chair in the lecture hall, resting my head on my arm, struggling to keep my eyes open. Professor Carney looked as if he didn't get much sleep either, but then again, I'm sure it's hard to seem enthusiastic about the same topic after teaching it for twenty plus years. Me being the over achiever that I am, I conveniently picked the seat that is in the center of the lecture hall in the third row, which didn't help because if you had an off day, much like today, the professor would surely notice.

I stared blankly into the slideshow presentation projected on the big screen. Today's topic: Cannibalistic Organisms. Great. The topic of animals eating their own kind was only adding insult to injury, after the nightmare I just had. The irony felt like life was mocking me in some cruel way.

With a click of his keyboard, Professor Carney moved to the next slide, and ofcourse it would be of giant black widow spider. As a reflex at the sight of the spider I threw my head back and moaned.

Time stood still. I realized that I was much louder than I had aimed to be. The class became quieter than usual. Professor Carney turned his attention to me. I could feel the gaze of my fellow students surrounding me.

"Uhh- sorry I'm scared of spiders" I explained humorously. It was a lie but I had to think on my feet.

Professor Carney grinned, humoring my reasoning. "It's okay D'Angelo, the spider won't hurt you." He continued on with his lecture maintaining the smirk on his face.

I hope so, I thought.

A subtle burst of positive energy traveled throughout the lecture hall. I think we all needed a joke to put us in a good energized spirit to help us through the lecture.

Just as I was beginning to relax and forget about my problems back at home, my phone in my pocket vibrated. I didn't think much of it. It was probably my mom who was in Florida texting me good morning as she usually does or something. But I remembered she had already texted me good morning while I was riding the 4 train to school. A knot had formed in my throat as my intuition was preparing me for who I dreaded it not to be.

I slowly reached into my pocket and pulled out my phone and read a text message from Milly. It was indeed the message I did not want to receive.

911.

I sunk into my chair and threw my head back. *Are you kidding me?* I thought. It's only been a couple of hours since leaving Milly back at home, how much trouble could she be in? I was tired and was in no mood to deal with Milly's bullshit. *She's a big girl, she can fix her own mess.* I tucked my phone back into my pocket and refocused on the slideshow.

I was good at getting inside my own head, too much sometimes even. Sometimes overthinking helped save my ass, other times it added unnecessary stress to my life. As seconds turned into a few minutes, I slowly conjured more and more scenarios in my head, fueling my anxiety. It wasn't long before I started to spiral. What *if she went to the witch again? What if she is slowly dying? What if something happened to my grandma? Son of a bitch!*

I snatched my bookbag off the floor and placed it on my lap. I then swiped my phone from my pocket and placed it inside my bookbag so Professor Carney wouldn't see me texting.

What happened? Are you okay? I texted.

The seconds felt like minutes and minutes felt like hours. *If it's a real emergency she would've responded by now,* I thought. I became jittery, waiting for her reply. I turned and shifted in my seat, the anxiety set into my stomach, giving me an acid burning sensation. After a few minutes I texted Milly again. *HELLO, WHAT'S UP?* I texted.

What if the witch got her? Or she's been attacked by the demon that was chasing me! I thought, *and that's why she's not answering!*

The jitters spread down into my leg, which began to bounce like I had a double espresso shot. My right hand, holding my phone, became numb.

Finally I got a response. *Meet me outside your building,* Milly wrote.

What kind of fucked-up response is that? I asked myself. No detail, no answer to me asking what was wrong, just *meet me outside your building.*

I had about another 15 minutes to go before class was dismissed. I could leave early, but I would stick out more than I already was. My nerves surely made me look like I was paranoid that a bomb was about to go off.

I jot down some notes from the presentation, not internalizing a damn thing, just playing it off. Writing something down was just a way to exercise the nerves running through my body.

After a grueling ten minutes, Professor Carney came to the end of his slide show. Knowing professor Carney, he'll end the class early after finishing the presentation. *Thank God!* I thought.

"That concludes today's lecture please be sure to-" *blah blah blah gotta go*, I voiced in my head. I'll get the homework from my friend, Bryan or something.

"I'll see you next week," Carney finished. I shoved my notebook into my bookbag and bolted to my left, the nearest aisle to the exit. Before reaching the aisle I almost immediately tripped and nearly fell to the floor. Thankfully I caught myself by grabbing the back of an empty chair ahead of me. I paused and awkwardly looked around and saw the expression on Professor Carney's concerned face. Others, some still in their chairs, watched on as they questioned what the hell was wrong with me. I gained my footing, circled in place apologizing for the cringey exit. "Sorry, sorry." I continued expeditiously up the stairway aisle. With any luck they'll just think I have a severe case of arachnophobia or something.

I burst through the door, exiting the lecture room to join a small sea of students parading in and out of their respective classes and destinations. I darted around each one, paying little mind to anyone in my proximity.

"Hey D'Angelo!" I heard behind me. It was my buddy Bryan who just left the lecture hall following me. "You okay?" he asked.

"I'm good, just gotta go brother!" I said, peering over the crowd spotting his face in the mix. I continued with my head turned backward, not wanting to cause anymore concern to my good friend Bryan.

Without paying attention to anything in front of me, I made a right down a hallway, and accidentally bumped into someone, knocking their books out of their hands. Without hesitation I felt guilty and kneeled down to retrieve the fallen books.

"I'm so sorry," I apologized. "I didn't see you there."

I looked ahead and saw dark blue stretch jeans in my field of view. The person whom I knocked into kneeled down to my level. A veil of dark curly hair shrouded the woman's face. I paused in awe, as the voluminous mane seemed all too familiar and alluring. She finally looked up and matched my gaze. It was Jessica.

I didn't need to break the eye contact we shared at that moment to know the school of students thinned out from around us. Her presence gave me a shot of bliss, that calmed the rapid flow of anxiety into mere ripples, and those ripples into the stillness. Her beauty, her presence, her aura, was exactly what I needed.

"It's okay D'Angelo!" she said while picking up one of her books.

"Yeah I'm just in a rush" I replied while giving her the other book I've retrieved from the floor.

"You in a rush?" she asked.

"Um nah-, I mean a little bit-, just gotta help a friend. A friend who needs my help." *Smooth.*

My attempt at sounding cool and well put together cracked a smile on her face. "Okay D'Angelo, always being

Spider-Man swinging to the rescue I see. Don't forget to let Peter Parker have some rest."

We both stood up straight.

"Being Spider-Man is a tough job- yeah" I said. "But I'll try." I noticed a scratch on the side of her forehead, just peeking out from her curly hair.

"What's that?" I asked.

She almost immediately knew what I was talking about as she went to gently tap the red streak. "Oh- the scratch? Yeah- last night got a little crazy at the party after you left" she explained.

"Got into a fight?" I asked.

"No Mr. Spider-Man, just some drunk college kids partying too hard." She explained.

"Oh okay, that's good. It was nice dancing with you by the way."

"Same, I told you you could do it!"

"Yeah we should do it again sometime"

"I'll be down for that" she replied with a big smile.

"Awesome-."

For some reason, an image of Milly flashed in my mind, and I remembered what I was in a rush for.

"Uh well I'll see you around! I continued "we'll catch up!"

"Okay!"

"Gotta go save the day!" I joked.

"Okay Spidey!"

To humor the whole Spider-Man comparison I gestured shooting webs from my wrist and pretending to swing away.

My child-like playful nature plastered a big smile on her face. Call me what you want, corny, wack, goofy, it didn't matter. Girls like Jessica accepted and appreciated me for who I was which only made her even more wonderful.

I quickly abandoned my playful exit and rushed down the hallway, and made my way to the double doors exiting the building. With a fresh image of Jessica in my mind, and hearing her endearing words comparing me to Spider-Man, I felt like I was ready for anything life had to throw at me. Boy, was I wrong.

Chapter
EIGHT

TEN OF CUPS — REVERSED

With time being of the essence, I took an Uber instead of the hour-and-a-half train ride back home. Upon arrival I saw Milly standing at the end of my street with wide eyes, looking a little paranoid.

"Right here is good, thank you!" I told the Uber driver. I hastily exited the car and closed the door behind me.

"What happened?" I asked Milly.

"How was school?" she replied with a humorous tone. She does this when she doesn't wanna talk about something she did wrong. Now was not the time for games.

"Milly, for real, what happened?" I said with frustration.

She paused as she knew I meant business.

"I might've hurt someone"

"Hurt someone? What do you mean?"

"I might have killed someone."

I paused as I was dumbfounded with what she just said.

"What the hell do you mean you think you killed someone?" I asked. "You either did or you didn't—I think you would know—"

"Shh!" Milly snapped, grabbing my shoulders.

"The reason I'm not sure is because I don't remember any of it," she said in a hushed tone. "I was walking home and this guy stopped me, we were making out, next thing I knew I was standing over him and he—" Milly began to choke on her words. "—he had his throat ripped out and there was blood everywhere!"

I soon became overwhelmed with all the information she was bombarding me with, making my skin crawl and lungs heavy. The image of her making out with a random guy, and becoming a murder suspect, all within a couple of hours is troubling and perplexing to say the least. She has to hold the world record for doing the absolute most in a 24 hour span. And I'm the dumbass who's been an accessory to nearly all of it.

Part of me hoped she was lying or at the very least hallucinating.

"Okay, slow down Milly if you killed someone, anyone, especially ripping their throat out, there would be blood all over you. Where's the blood?" I asked.

"I don't know, I looked down and he was lying in his bed naked." she replied.

"Why was he naked?"

"I-"

"Matter of fact, don't answer that!" The thought of Milly having sex with someone would bother the 13 year old boy inside of me.

"Maybe none of that happened. We had a crazy night last night, you know? Stress and a lack of proper sleep could—"

A bloodcurdling scream came from behind me. Milly looked past my right shoulder and focused her attention across the street. I reluctantly turned to see what was the matter.

A plump middle aged woman in a green floral dress rushed down the block. Her hands were propped up by her side, showing her metallic red palms. She cried desperately to another woman walking up the block with tote bags filled with groceries.

"Mi hijo! Mi hijo!" the woman cried.

The other woman dropped her tote bags in horror, covering her mouth momentarily before catching the bloodied mother who fell to her knees. Her cries sent shockwaves throughout the neighborhood.

One by one windows began to open from the apartment building across the street. People looked down from their fire escapes with grave concern. Others exited from shops such as the deli store and laundromat to join in on investigating the painful cry. They inched toward the mother, circling her like a horde of zombies. Few consoled her, others continued to look on from a distance.

I watched on, deeply disturbed, but I couldn't look away. It was like watching a horror movie, except I was now in it.

Not only am I starring in it, but the person whom I loved deeply was the killer, the culprit, the monster. The tears, the blood, the pain, the horror in everyone's face leaving me stricken with guilt. You don't have to be the one holding the knife to be responsible for someone's death.

I turned my attention to Milly, who looked on with remorse and criminality in her eyes.

My despair and guilt grew into anger. There was only one person to blame for this atrocious matter. Milly is an easy person to point the finger at, but I knew the true culprit, and was the only person who could fix this.

Madam Maria.

Chapter

NINE

FIVE OF CUPS

I marched up Westchester Avenue ready to take matters into my own hands. I paid no mind to the fact that I was now backpedaling to where I once ran for my life the night before. Pressing through the cold wind, I trampled the fallen tree branches and garbage bags that were in my way.

Police and EMT sirens echoed in the distance. Two cop cars sped past me and Milly heading towards my street. The entire neighborhood probably knows what happened by now.

Milly reluctantly followed with pouting lips and her arms crossed like a child. With Madam Maria's house now in sight Milly broke the silence.

"D'Angelo, I don't think we should go inside," she protested.

"It's a little late to think that, don't you think?"

"No! D! Listen—"

I snapped around in anger. "Milly, I know whatever witchcraft she did last night caused this. None of this makes sense! And this is not a coincidence! This happened because of her!" I snapped back around and pushed past the iron gate. "—If she can do this, she can undo this—or something!"

Before taking a step up the stoop, I felt something different, freezing me in my tracks. I looked to the ground and saw shards of glass beneath a window to my left, which belonged to Madam Maria's living room.

"Was the glass always there?" I asked Milly.

"No I don't think so."

I spent most of my time last night in Madam Maria's living room, and didn't notice the window was broken. Seeing Madam Maria's house in the daylight allowed me to see just how run down it truly was.

"It's open," Milly said.

I turned my attention to the front door, and it was indeed cracked open a few inches.

After examining the new troubling details of the house, I began reassessing the situation. My anger and focus on confronting Madam Maria began to subside. Just when I thought I knew what I was walking into, the pieces on the board had shifted. Something happened last night after we left, but what?

I pulled the front door open and perched my leg on the top step holding it open. I looked down the dark hallway that led deeper into Madam Maria's house. No light or sign of life in sight, only some leaves and Madam Maria's pamphlet papers littered the floor.

"Hello? Madam Maria?" I called.

I looked back at Milly, who paid no mind to me, instead her attention was locked on the dark tunneling mystery that laid ahead.

"We're coming in!" I announced. I lunged up the steps, holding the door open for Milly to follow me. This time, Milly looked more concerned than me for once.

As we made our way deeper into the hallway foyer, hazy sunlight peeked around the bend from the living room.

Turning the corner, I was alarmed by the state the living room was in. The white sunlight protruding from the broken window showed the aftermath of what looked like a tornado. The dingy, dark-blue carpet was trashed with broken glass, books, newspapers, and pamphlets. The shelves, once lined with books, trinkets and decor were now empty. Only dust and cobwebs remained.

I surveyed the room, trying to make sense of what happened. The more I looked around the room the more I grew confused and concerned. Something bad definitely happened, as if someone unleashed hell after we left.

To my right was the closed door belonging to the Enchanting Room. I was far too scared to open it. Instead I called out once more in hopes to get a response.

"Madam Maria, I know you're in here. We need you to reverse whatever you did last night! It's an emergency."

I paused, hoping to hear a response but the house stayed silent.

"Was it like this when we came last night?" Milly asked. "I can actually see everything now."

"No," I answered. "I was here when you were with her. The window wasn't broken, and pretty much everything that was on the floor was on the shelves or the desk."

"There has to be something that can help us." Milly said while stepping forward. She looked down, perusing the cluttered mess of newspapers and pamphlets on the floor, until something caught her eye. She kneeled down and fixated on one particular newspaper.

"Minnesota Teen Ripped Apart," she read aloud. "What the fuck?" she murmured.

Within the cluttered mess surrounding us, something stuck out to me. On the desk lay the same brown leather journal from the night before. Its presence was odd as it seemed to be the only thing to have survived the cyclone that ripped through here.

"Mill," I called.

"Yeah?"

"This is the same journal I saw last night," I explained. "Don't you think it's weird how it's the only thing not out of place?"

"Maybe she put it there before leaving." Milly answered. "But maybe it'll tell us how to fix this or where she'll be at!"

Milly eagerly reached for the book before I raised my hand, halting her.

"Woah, woah, woah!" I said. "If there's one thing I've learned from horror movies, Milly, it's that you do not take a witch's book!"

"Really?" she asked with an annoyed face.

"Yeah really! You either end up dead, or turn into a cat! And from the looks of it anything is possible."

"Then what do you suggest we do?"

I paused and stared at the book, weighing my options. This suspicious journal was the only lead we had to finding Madam Maria and fixing whatever was wrong with Milly. Maybe the journal would have something that could tell us where she could be, maybe an address, phone numbers or anything. I caved in.

"I guess you're right, we can at least try."

In defeat, I rested my palm on the journal gripping the edges, but before I was able to lift it, a loud creaking sound erupted behind us. I snatched my hand off the journal as if I had touched fire. Simultaneously, we turned around and set our sights on the door that led to the enchanting room and then back at each other. No words were spoken, yet we understood what the other was thinking.

In an attempt to test to see what would happen, I lightly placed my hand on top of the journal once again, yet another deep creek sounded from the enchanting room. In fear I snatched my hand off once again.

Whatever was on the other side of the door was big. But worse of all, it wasn't Madam Maria, it was guarding the journal, and it knew we were in the house.

I was prepared to leave the journal as it was and head for the exit but before I could step, Milly grabbed hold of the steering wheel in her usual fashion.

"Madam Maria?" She said while stepping towards the door.

"What the fuck are you doing?" I whispered.

Milly snapped her head around and pressed her index finger against her lips, hushing me. She inched her way to the door, step by step and reached out for the door knob.

I protested the idea while standing in place behind her, flailing my arms in a desperate attempt to signal to her to not open the door. I remembered with Milly, sometimes you have to use reverse psychology if you want her to do something. If you want her to do something, tell her to do the opposite, and usually you'll get what you wanted all along. It's a trick I've learned over the years, but in the heat of the moment, such as now, I would forget.

"Milly don't you dare—" I said in a hushed tone. "Milly please—why? Why are you like this?" My vocal cords began to strain from how I was whispering and yelling at the same time.

Milly gripped the door knob and pushed it open with her shoulder. She stood there frozen

looking inside the room. I watched on, clenching my jaw, assuming the worst was in the room, preparing to attack her and then me.

She looked back at me, wide-eyed like a deer in head-lights and shook her head no.

"Nothing?" I asked.

"Nothing." Milly confirmed. She then stepped back into the living room and closed the door behind her.

"Then what the hell made that noise?"

"I don't know—" Milly's face became rigid with fear as the floorboards creaked once more from behind the door.

"What is it?" I asked.

A shadow from under the door caught my attention, silencing me. The sound of the front door slamming shut sent chills up my spine. There was no denying something was in the house with us.

Milly and I knew we wore out our welcome and it was time for us to go. Milly peeked around the corner to look down the foyer to the entrance of the house. She held up her hands holding five fingers up. She then held up four.

I got the message that she was counting down to make a run for the exit. I took a deep breath in and braced myself.

Three fingers.

I placed my right leg behind me, preparing to sprint. A lump in my throat emerged and my mouth became dry.

Two fingers.

The nerves were settling in. I took one last look at the leather journal. I wasn't sure what would be our next move after leaving this journal behind. I turned my attention back to Milly who was also preparing to run just as I am, but the anticipation excited her as she looked back at me with a big smile, like we're two kids playing tag. Only her.

One finger.

Without much thought, I bolted to Milly. By the time I reached the corner to exit the living room, I could see the door to the Enchanting Room swing open in my peripheral vision. I nearly ran into Milly who was only a couple of steps ahead of me.

"Go! Go!" I yelled.

"Shit, shit, shit, shit—" Milly murmured under her breath.

As we ran for our lives down the narrow foyer, I felt footsteps stomping followed by the sound of deep grunts behind me. I was too terrified to look back and face whatever it was. I was convinced that If I were to hesitate for a single second I'd be as good as dead.

Milly busted open the front door, falling to the ground. Just before I was able to reach the sunlight, something had grabbed a hold of my ankle, sending me toppling forward.

"Milly!" I called, reaching out my hand.

Milly looked back and saw me in trouble. She crawled up the steps and grabbed my hand.

"Hold on!" Milly shouted while standing up.

I began to feel my lower half lift off the ground. *What the hell got me?* I thought. Despite me being terrified, I couldn't help but look at what was holding onto me. I looked down at my feet in the air and saw nothing more but the empty dark foyer. It was clear that whatever has a hold of me wasn't part of this world.

Milly wasn't letting go of me, I was surprised she had this much upper body strength. I don't think I've ever seen

Milly work out a day in her life, yet she's playing tug of war with an invisible entity and using me as the rope. At that moment I didn't care how or why, I just wanted her to win.

Just as I began to lose feeling in my right leg, the demon lost its grip and sent Milly and I flying out the door. As she fell backwards I cupped the back of her head to take the impact of the concrete floor below. I couldn't do much about my body weight landing on top of her. She groaned in pain. I rolled off of her and took a deep breath, relieved to be out of the house. I tilted my head up and saw the front door wide open, still not able to see the monster inside.

Footsteps echoed from inside the house, closing in on us. I sat up and pleaded for mercy with my one hand halting the invisible being.

"No! No, No!"

The footsteps stopped. I paused in suspense, bracing myself for another round of fighting for my life but instead the front door slammed shut. I lay back down, exhausted, joining Milly in gasping for air.

"Thank You! Thank You! You're my favorite demon" I wheezed. With the little bit of strength I had left, I rolled over and gave her a peck on the forehead. Even though I wouldn't be in this mess if it wasn't for her, she still just saved my life.

"Oh shut up" she giggled, while pushing me off. "Are you okay?"

"Yeah-" I stood up and reached my hand down and helped her off the floor. "I think so, I might need therapy after all this but, yeah, you?"

"Yeah- too bad we didn't see Madam Maria, or get anything that could help us"

"Speak for yourself." I smirked and reached into my pants pocket. I pulled out the journal that was on Madam Maria's desk. I held it up like it was a gift.

"Oh my god no way! You did it!" She looked up at me in amazement. "You got the Journal!" she said, throwing her arms up and hugging me, pulling me down to her height.

For a split second, it almost made it seem like it was all worth it. Once again I felt invincible—masculine, appreciated, and dare I say, heroic?

A deep bellowing growl came from behind the door, snapping us out of our tender moment.

"Yeah we should go," I said startled.

"Yeah!"

We shuffled in place before pushing past the iron gate and began power-walking down the street. We didn't look back. If we left something behind, it belongs to the invisible demon now.

The neighborhood greeted us with heavy traffic, car horns, and blaring sirens in all directions. I didn't do anything, but I felt like I was a wanted man and the police could want me for questioning. I'm with the suspected killer after all. I was reluctant to look over at Milly beside me, instead I continued to power-walk ahead and speak loudly enough for her to hear.

"Okay Milly, we gotta lay low for a couple of days, until we get things straight okay?"

"Yeah—Yeah no problem!"

As we continued on our way, I became lost in my own thoughts; questioning what the hell just happened? And where do we go from here? The horror movies I used to watch weren't lying apparently, but nothing could have prepared me for this and everything that is yet to come.

Chapter
TEN

JUSTICE

Thankfully the past few days have been calmer. Nothing out of the ordinary besides the neighborhood crawling with cops, investigating the gruesome murder that happened up the street from me. A squad car was parked at both ends of the block and an occasional helicopter would fly past the neighborhood. Investigators would stop people in the neighborhood and question them, asking if they had seen anything suspicious or knew the victim.

I was hesitant to watch the local news and hear the details of what exactly happened, but by the next day, you would literally have had to be living under a rock to avoid the startling truth. After overhearing bits and pieces at school, the deli store, and on social media, I decided to turn on the local news, and see what information they had on the matter. Just after their short story on a local food pantry, the female news anchor appeared on the screen.

"Breaking news, in a developing story of a Bronx resident murdered in their bedroom is now being identified-"

Unable to turn away, my jaw clenched with anxiety. My leg twitched uncontrollably. I was preparing for the worst.

"—The victim has now been identified as twenty-three-year-old Joshua Bautista." Beside the news anchor, showed a picture of him with a large curly afro, an afro that looked familiar.

My jaw dropped when I recognized the victim's face and hair. It was that asshole Joshua from the other night! The same one that was harassing Milly! But how? When? Why? I was confused as much as I was shocked. After a moment of being baffled, I turned my attention back to the TV and saw a news reporter standing outside in a tan trench coat holding a microphone, speaking to the camera.

"—The victim was found just last Saturday afternoon by his mother, who walked into his room and discovered her son in a pool of his own blood. A large portion of the victim's throat was ripped out, with deep cuts and lacerations around the upper torso and arms. Medical personnel pronounced the victim dead at the scene."

My neck and shoulders became stiff, making it nearly unbearable to sit still. Just as I was praying for this past weekend to be only a fever dream, I was slowly being dragged back into the hellish nightmare. Who would I be able to go to for help? It was all too out of this world for anyone to believe me. I took a sip of my Pepsi to help moisten my dry mouth and clear the lump in my throat.

The news began to show highlights of the press conference, showing The police chief, Charlie Vega, dressed in all black uniform speaking at a podium in a room full of reporters.

"As I said earlier, this is an ongoing investigation. We're about 48 hours removed from finding the body of the victim, there will be further developments as the evidence begins to unfold," he said. "What I can say is that Joshua Bautista was a beloved son and family member, and was tragically killed, so our thoughts and prayers go out to his family and friends," he continued. The police chief looks out into the audience and the room becomes dead silent. The police chief points a finger out into the crowd.

"Yes?"

I couldn't hear the question, but the police chief apparently hears him just fine.

"We don't have any suspects at this time. We have asked dozens of people and nobody

saw Joshua that morning or afternoon with anybody," the police chief answered.

Thank God I thought. Last thing I needed to hear was *Joshua was seen walking with a cute curly-haired girl*. Despite Milly claiming to loosely remember the events leading up to seeing Joshua dead in front of her, my gut told me she might be responsible. My undying optimism, and logical thinking held on for hope that there was a non-incriminating and reasonable explanation for Milly's story.

"You in the back!" the police chief said. "Yes."

Another muffled voice sounded in the distance. The Police chief stood still waiting for the reporter to finish his question, nodding his head.

"At the moment, there is no particular weapon—" The police chief paused and looked

down, wiping his face. He looked almost unsure of what to say next. "At the moment, investigators are pointing to teeth and claws as the initial weapons used to kill Joshua-"

The room erupted with the reporters gasping and chatting amongst themselves. Camera flashes flickered, nearly blinding the police chief as he shielded his eyes. The disruption seemed to have hit a nerve, possibly making him regret his statement.

"Pipe down! Everybody relax!" he demanded.

The tension in the room began to simmer down, as the reporters regained composure, allowing him to continue.

"Again it's not definite, but it's a lead for now. The trauma caused to Joshua's neck is believed to have been caused by teeth of a canine or a large animal. The scratches surrounding the torso and arms of the victim don't seem to belong to any knife or object at the moment. It is possible, again not definite, that a person who had control of a large animal, whom Joshua knew, walked into the house and was attacked by the animal or even a rabid dog."

The mass of reporters again erupted in hysteria. The police chief leaned back and waved his hand vigorously in front of his face, shooing away the flashes of light and hushing the overwhelmingly loud crowd before him.

"Okay! Okay! Listen here!" He shouted.

The energy from the crowd had died down, not fully, but just enough for the police chief to speak out clearly.

"We will find the individual or individuals responsible for this! There will be justice for Joshua, Thank you!" The police chief took a step back and looked to his left behind him, receiving a nod from his colleagues before walking off the stage.

I muted the TV and tossed the remote to my bed and turned away. Part of me was

relieved that the evidence pointed to a large animal as the killer, and the owner lost control of it. Neither me or Milly have had a dog or mountain lion on a leash, so in the eyes of the police department, we're innocent. But that doesn't discredit the alarming fact that Milly was actually there at the scene of the crime, and what's even scarier is the fact that Milly is indeed the rabid dog the police were looking for. If Milly did tear Joshua to shreds, something demonic had to be inside of her to make her do it.

Madam Maria's journal caught my attention as it lay there on my computer desk. I haven't turned more than a few pages due to the fear that I might make matters worse or find something that I would regret.

I was tempted now more than ever to dive head first into Madam Maria's journal and find a clue to reverse whatever spell she casted on Milly, but I was reminded of something very important. Ricky! I remembered that Joshua was

Ricky's cousin. I must've seemed like such a douchebag for not reaching out and sending my condolences to him and his family. That explains why I haven't seen him around at school today. Now that I think about it, I haven't seen him on social media either. But would it be adding insult to injury knowing that I know who is responsible for his death and not saying anything? Yeah, I'm in deep douchebag territory.

I was conflicted to reach out and call him, but I couldn't look any worse than I already had the few days for not reaching out. Me and Ricky were really good friends, homies since meeting freshman year, if anybody should be there for him it should be me.

I called Ricky and anxiously waited for him to answer. With each ring, I felt as if I was stepping closer to a ticking time bomb. He could know it was Milly, he could be crying hysterically, he could be upset that I'm just reaching out to him now. A part of me silently begged him not to answer. I wasn't sure of what to say. I have never been in this situation before.

"Hello?" Ricky said, followed by a sniffle. I could hear some Spanish rap music in the background.

"Hey brody!" I said. "I uh—I just wanted to check up on you, and send you my condolences for your lost brother man."

All I could hear was the phone shuffling around on his end, and then the music stopped playing in the background. I didn't hear anything. I wanted to give him a moment to respond, but instead, a moment of silence passed.

"Hello?" I asked.

"Yeah bro, thank you."

Ricky wasn't his cheerful self, which was completely understandable, but I know I had to dig a little deeper and force him to talk and say anything that was on his mind. Again I was reluctant to push forward and get him talking, but I had to, as a friend.

"yeah—how are you holding up? You know I'm here for you if you need me."

Suddenly my phone vibrated from receiving a text. I looked down and saw a text message from Milly.

Hey D'Angelo, whatcha doin? She wrote with a smiley face emoji.

I was in no mood to talk to Milly. She's been normal the last few days, at least in my eyes and I would like to keep it that way as best as I can. I could hear Ricky speaking again so I put the phone back to my ear.

"Yeah, I know bro, thank you." His voice sounded sluggish, like he was slurring his words. "You know bro, if you're not busy you can come over and talk."

I took that as a cry for help. My choices were to either hang out with my friend who's possessed by a demon or help my grieving friend, mourning the loss of his cousin who was murdered. I chose the road less stressful and accepted his invitation.

"Yeah, Ricky I'm free, of course. You at your place?" I asked.

"Yeah, you know where to find me."

We said our goodbyes and hung up. Ricky sounded drunk, possibly drowning his sorrows in a bottle of Don Julio knowing him.

I slipped into some clothes and threw on my lucky leather jacket, all while resisting the urge to text Milly back as I normally would. Hopefully she'll just think I'm busy doing homework or asleep or something.

AFTER A SHORT RIDE ON THE 6 TRAIN, I HAD ARRIVED at Ricky's house that night. He lived in a nice small multi-family house with a garage and a tall stoop. The rest of his neighborhood was quiet and dark, but not Ricky's house. Much like his exuberant nature, his brightly lit garage and loud music made his house stand out from the rest on the block like a beacon.

I noticed the garage door wide open and latin music blasting from it. I walked over and found Ricky in the center, sitting on a metal folding chair, with a red plastic cup by his foot. He had his back turned to the garage door, so he wasn't able to notice me. I didn't want to spook him so I walked inside the garage and spoke firmly so he could hear me.

"Ricky!" I called. I got no response, but he did begin to sway slightly in rhythm with the music. "Ricky!" I tried again. This time he paused and began to look over his shoulder. "Ricky! Bro!" I said, finally catching his attention. He turned around and his squinted droopy eyes widened when he saw me.

"Hey, bro, what's up?" he said while standing to greet me. He gave me a weak dap handshake and hug welcoming me. The strong stench of alcohol off of his brown sweater irritated my nose. For a moment I felt his body weight resting on me for support so he wouldn't fall over. "Come in, bro! Have a seat if you want." He pointed to the same seat he just got up from.

I quickly surveyed the garage and found that was the only seat available. I figured that he needed the seat more than me, so I declined.

"I'm good, thanks!"

Ricky paid me no mind and staggered over to the large speakers in the back of the garage. He rested his arm on top of the speakers as if to take a second to regain his balance, before turning the music down low enough for us to talk. He then turned to me and leaned against the speaker. Seeing him standing there with his red glassy eyes was honestly hard to look at. I've seen him drunk before, but this was a different kind of drunk.

"How—you been bro?" he asked.

"I've been good, just wanted to check up on you, you know?"

I'm used to being the sober one in group outings. I'm also use to being the guy people would come and talk to about their problems, but I've never helped someone during a drunk grieving period before. With Ricky towering over me, I became worried about what to exactly expect. Ricky would easily over power me if he became belligerent or violent even. I had to pick my words carefully, get his mind off of things if I could.

"I appreciate it." Ricky looked off to the side as if he was annoyed. There was a good chance he had been saying that over the last few days to everybody who had reached out. A moment of silence between the two of us passed. I remembered Ricky had a nice white Honda car that once belonged to his uncle.

"So where's your whip? Did someone steal it?" I said jokingly.

"Nah, my mom and sister went to go see my aunt at the hospital."

"Why? What happened to her?" I asked.

"You know, ever since my cousin got murdered, she's been having panic attacks—lashing out and stuff."

Fuck I thought. I tried to steer the conversation to something else but walked right into what I was trying to avoid. It became a little more awkward for me. All I could picture was Joshua's mom, Ricky's aunt, screaming and hollering about the house, probably in the psych ward from all the stress. I can't blame her. Finding your son with their throat ripped out would cause anybody's parents to have a mental breakdown.

"Oh. I'm sorry to hear that." That was all I could say as I looked to the ground. I was unable to make eye contact with Ricky as I apologized.

"Yeah—It's crazy, you just met him the day before he— the day before it happened."

"Yeah, he was... something." 'Something' was the best word I was able to come up with at that moment. Joshua didn't give the best first impression to me and Milly at Ricky's party. Ricky chuckled at my response.

"Don't worry, I know, Joshua was an asshole, but he wasn't all the time." Ricky began slowly walking towards me. He bent over forward and picked up his red cup from off the floor. "The family really loved him though—I loved him." Ricky tilted his head back and gulped the last bit of his drink.

"Yeah, I'm sure you all did. And that was just one encounter, I'm sure he was a cool dude."

"Yeah, he was. But alcohol brings out the ugly," Ricky said, while shaking the empty red cup in my face. "I remember one time, back in May, for his birthday, homie got into a fight with his own friends over some bullshit. But they squashed that beef or whatever I think." He walked past me and started walking to the corner of the garage where a large punching bag was hanging from the ceiling. He tossed the cup to the floor before giving the punching bag a gentle blow.

"So do you guys have any idea who did it?" I asked.

"No," he said, without shifting his focus away from the punching bag. He gave it another blow, but this time with enough force to push it back a couple of inches. "Doesn't matter. I'm going to find whoever did it."

For a moment, I felt guilty, knowing that I'm part of the reason his cousin died the way he did, and yet I'm here in his garage, playing stupid. Despite Ricky's grief and anger,

I doubted he would find out who actually killed his cousin, let alone get himself tangled in this paranormal web of a mess. So instead of brushing off his belief in finding the killer, I encouraged him, like a good friend would.

"I'm sure you will bro." I responded. "The police are going to find out who did it."

Ricky was now facing off with the punching bag in a fighting stance as if he was in a professional boxing ring, paying me no attention.

"Fuck the police!" Ricky said while he threw a couple of stiff punches. "I'm going to find that son of a bitch myself."

Ricky looked at the punching bag more menacingly, as if he saw the killer standing in front of him. He landed a few more jabs, each one harder than the last. Ricky started to work up a sweat as he started to become out of breath and his forehead began to glisten. Ricky paused for a moment to catch his breath. He grabbed the chain above the punching bag, using it as support to hold him up while he rested.

"I'm already working on finding the bastard, I got people helping me and shit" he said while panting.

"What do you mean? How?" I asked.

"You know, my neighborhood is gonna help keep an eye out for anything suspicious. Plus you're not going to believe this bro!"

"I doubt it, go ahead" I replied.

Ricky turned to me and rested his hands on his waist, taking a deep breath in, "I'm telling you bro, god finds a way to send you his messengers!"

"Yeah I agree."

"Okay, the other day when my aunt stayed the night over here, I had to step outside and take a break from all the crying and stuff going on here, I was overwhelmed. I took a walk a few blocks away, and this old lady who was standing in an alleyway called me. She walked over to me and she asked if I was okay. Come to find out she was a psychic medium bro!"

An alarm went off in my head. An image of Madam Maria's smile stained my vision, snapping my focus away from Ricky. This wasn't a mere coincidence, she knew what she was doing, but the fact Madam Maria is trying to target Ricky only shows me she's still alive and I haven't escaped her grasp just yet. I needed more information from Ricky, but I couldn't lead him to suspect anything was wrong or that I knew the same psychic medium who was really a witch.

"Oh really?" I squealed. "What did—what did she say?"

"Well that's the weird part, because she sounded like she already knew what was happening or how I felt. I told her I was just dealing with some family issues, as she gave me her condolences!"

"Oh that's weird I responded." *Yeah this is definitely Madam Maria* I thought. She did the same thing with me and Milly when we first met her. But I feared for what was said or done after their initial greeting. "So how did she help you?"

"She told me to take charge and get my revenge on those who betrayed me and lied to me and to avenge my cousin, cause that's what he would want me to do. She offered to do a tarot reading but before I could get her contact info my little sister was calling me down the block, she was looking for me. When I turned around, she was gone."

Ricky couldn't read my mind, but I was thanking god a thousand times over. Lord knows what she would've done to Ricky had she had the chance to lure him in. She'd probably possess him too or tell him the real truth of what happened.

"Yeah, that's crazy man. But aren't you religious? Wouldn't even participating in that be against your beliefs?" I asked.

Ricky took a deep breath and exhaled.

"I am, but mediums and fortune tellers are not uncommon in hispanic culture. A lot of people frown upon it, but sometimes it's the last resort to solve your problems, you know? As for right now I just needed to be pointed in the right direction." He turned back to the punching bag and began striking again. "I don't know who it is, but they're gonna get what's coming to them!"

It was getting late and although Ricky didn't directly threaten me or Milly, I felt as if it was time to go. Part of me wanted to tell Ricky the truth, but I didn't want to be the one to tell a belligerent Ricky that Milly is possessed by a demon and killed his cousin. He'd either beat me up, call the cops, harm Milly, or I would end up in a loony bin somewhere.

"Yeah I get it bro, I get it. I'ma head home—but listen, I hope you find that guy. I'm here if you need me okay?"

"Appreciate it bro- Thanks." Ricky gave me a dap hand-shake, followed by a brotherly hug. But before he fully let me go out of his grasp, he took a step back and grabbed both of my shoulders and looked down upon me. "And if you hear anything, or find out who it was, please tell me, okay?"

I looked up at Ricky's glassy eyes and saw how serious and desperate he really was. This was probably my last chance to come clean and tell him the truth. I felt guilty just breathing in his presence, withholding the truth from him. I couldn't look him in the eyes for too long, instead I just smiled and looked off to the side, trying to play it cool.

"You got it brother," I said, while patting his shoulder to let me go of his clutches.

He finally released me, dropping his arms to his sides. I turned and walked towards the open garage door. I felt his eyes piercing me in the back of my head yet I refused to look back. "Goodnight Bro!" I said as I stepped outside.

"Hey wait!" Ricky called.

I paused, and thought I had been caught, possibly in a lie, or maybe Ricky wasn't done interrogating me. I hesitantly turned around.

"Yeah?"

Ricky stood there with a smirk on his face, not saying anything.

"How's Milly by the way?"

I was hoping to leave her out of this conversation entirely. It would be nice to erase her from Ricky's memory, but I've spoken too much about her in the past with him to not make it a part of our usual small talks. At this moment, the less I say and the more vague the better.

"She's good, she's good, thanks. She's busy doing... Milly stuff, you know?"

Ricky nodded his head in approval.

"And what about Jessica? Have you taken her out on a date yet?" he asked.

"Crap," I said under my breath. The thought of her brought a smile to my face. "Um, no, I've just been busy with all the essays and stuff for school, don't really have time to... you know?"

Ricky and I shared a chuckle.

"Alright man!" Ricky held up a peace sign as he walked towards the speakers in the back of his garage.

I turned my back and walked down his driveway. Ricky increased the volume of his music as I walked away. At the end of his driveway, I noticed a rolled-up piece of paper tied with a black string was tucked in the small chain linked fence. I looked back at Ricky who was preoccupied with the punching bag once again. I then looked to my sides, to see if the same rolled up piece of paper was in the neighboring house's front yards as well, but nothing. This rolled up letter was deliberately left for Ricky I concluded.

I carefully slid the paper out of the fence and began to look around, paranoid at the thought someone was watching me from the shadows. I pulled a loose end of the string, collapsing the knot like a gift. As I unraveled the paper, I saw the same haunting printed lettering as Madam Maria's pamphlets. At the top of the message, it read: *Madam Maria:*

Master of the Unknown, followed by her trademark symbol, the black crystal ball with an eye in the center of it. Beneath the symbol, what would be where she'd place her contact information, was blank.

I guessed Madam Maria was hanging low for the time being. She was out of sight, but definitely not out of mind, nor out of reach apparently. Far enough to not be touched but close enough for her to get you, and her next target apparently was Ricky, but why?

I surveyed my surroundings once more, and saw the neighborhood motionless and dark. I crumpled the piece of paper into a ball, stuffed it into my jacket pocket and stormed off.

I was in fear the entire trip home, watching my back, expecting for something to pop out and get me, Milly, Madam Maria or something. But after spending some time overthinking and in fear of what was waiting for me around each corner, my visit to Ricky's house reminded me of my mission: save Milly and put an end to Madam Maria once and for all.

Chapter
ELEVEN

THE STAR

It's been a couple of days since I visited Ricky at his house and since then I've been doing a deep dive on demonology and witchcraft. Through the safety of my computer screen, I've learned a lot, but as I continued researching, the information I was uncovering became more frightening and disturbing. The research started out kid-friendly, house witch practices; protection spells using stones, dirt, plants, hair and such. Before I knew it, I was reading passages and seeing depictions of demons and ritual sacrifices. The images alone were enough for me to wonder if I was seeing things that were possibly forbidden or illegal.

That Friday morning, I woke up with an epiphany, to cleanse myself of demonic and negative energy. I went to my neighborhood church, a place I haven't been for a long while. I've never gone to church by myself; I only used to go with my mom and or grandmother when I was a kid and maybe a teenager once or twice. I figured now would be as good of a time as any to visit.

The small catholic church was pretty empty as I walked in through its large open doors. One aisle separated two columns of benches, each having several vacant rows. The place had a thick smoky aroma like frankincense and sage. As I stood in the back of the church I saw an elderly couple in the front row on the left aisle, and one elderly man in the middle row on the right aisle.

In spite of me basically playing hopscotch with a few demons and witches the past week, I didn't start to burn or melt so I figured I was still on God's good side.

I dipped my finger in the holy water stoup and crossed myself before I crept down the aisle and sat two rows behind the elderly man who sat alone. I was careful to not make a peep and be seen—partly because I didn't wanna disturb the other attendees alone time, nor did I want to have a conversation with someone. I too just wanted alone time with God.

I sat and admired the colorful stained glass windows surrounding the church's walls, each depicting a different saint. On the back wall laid a large life size statue of Jesus nailed to the cross. Its lifelike details reminded me of when I used to go to church as a kid, and how looking at the statue used to make me sad, and question how anyone could do such a thing to somebody? Especially him.

I leaned back in my seat and draped my arm over the backrest of the bench. I stared blankly ahead to the podium, and to the average person, they would think I was in deep thought or was zoning out, but instead I was praying. I don't fold my hands or close my eyes most times when I pray, never felt the need to. I prayed for my loved ones to be safe and healthy, My grandmother, Ricky, Jessica, and Milly. I also prayed for strength to defeat these evils, plaguing my life and harming the people I care most about.

I've been raised to believe God gives his toughest battles to his strongest warriors, And here I am trying to help my friend who is possessed by a murderous demon, and trying to take down my neighborhood witch, all with a five-page paper due next week for my U.S history class.

I sat there for roughly half an hour, contemplating my next move and hoping to be struck by a miracle of God or to be given a sign. The eerie silence of the church made me feel a little uncomfortable and gave me the inclination that it was time to go.

As I shifted my body around, and began to rise, the elderly man who was two rows ahead of me, slowly turned to his left and looked at me curiously, halting me from standing up. He was an African American man with a round face and a neatly trimmed gray beard.

I wondered why and how I caught his attention when I barely made any noise shifting around in my seat. Instinctually, when I locked eyes with him I gave a half awkward smile and nodded my head. He greeted me back with a full comforting smile as if he was pleased to see me.

"Oh!" he said smoothly. Followed by a "wow," raising his eyebrows.

I looked away and back at him, unsure if it was me who piqued his interest or someone behind me.

The elderly man turned to his right and steadily exited out of his row and made his way over and sat in front of me.

"My oh my, looky here," he said.

I was confused, I didn't know what was so interesting about me, and I don't remember meeting this man ever in my life. My focus twitched between his thick gray eyebrows and white shirt, trying to grasp at any details that might help jog my memory of him, but nothing. Instead I returned his wide smile with one of my own.

"Hello sir!" I responded.

The Elderly man shifted his body to the left and rested his elbow on the back of the church bench.

"How are you?" he asked eagerly.

His voice was low and soothing as if he was a jazz singer in his earlier days.

"I've been good, and you?"

He looked away slightly, and grinned as if he was holding back from laughing.

"You don't remember me, do you?"

I could have lied at that moment for the sake of being polite, but decided not to.

"No, I don't think I do," I answered.

"Oh that's okay, I remember you tho! You used to come here as a little boy with your mom and grandmother right?"

My eyes widened.

"Yeah, I did!" I confirmed.

"Yeah, little D'Angelo, how could I forget?" he cackled.

I wasn't sure what to say next as I was astonished he knew my name, and remembered me over the years. Lord knows how long it's been since I've been in this church. With his calming voice and welcoming positive energy, I would have thought I met Santa Claus himself.

"Yeah, that's me," I chuckled. "It's been a while since coming here, I know."

"That's okay, how's your grandmother Alice? She was here a few months ago."

"She's good, thank you. She's home now—sleeping."

"I remember she used to come here faithfully."

"Yeah ever since her vision totally went away a year ago she's been attending church less and less."

The elderly man looked away and scrunched his lip.

"Ah, I understand. But I know you take good care of her tho", he said confidently.

"I will try my best."

"Oh I know you do, and that's all we can do! But I remember you was all she used to talk about. I remember when you got accepted into college, she was bragging to everyone that her grandson is going to college."

The thought of grandma boasting about me to the other churchgoers brought me joy. I couldn't hold back my smile, as I can picture her mentioning me and my accomplishments to anyone who would listen. But that was my grandma.

"Hey-" He said, snapping me out of my brief daydream. "What brings you in today?"

I sure as hell wasn't about to explain that my friend was possessed by a demon and I was looking for help to fight a witch in the neighborhood. I'm not trying to give the man a heart attack. Either that or he'll think I'm the one that needs to see an exorcist. I had to choose my words carefully.

"Just thought I'd come and make an effort—for old times sake."

He leaned back and smirked at me, as if he was proud that I would say such a thing.

"Ah," he said. "That's wonderful to hear. We all could use a little tune up spiritually in today's world."

"You can say that again," I sighed.

"I said, we could all use a tune up!" he repeated himself.

We burst out laughing. I looked over my shoulder to make sure we didn't disturb anyone else in the church. The elderly couple to our left paid us no mind.

"I get what you mean."

He cleared his throat after composing himself.

"But seriously, the evil in today's world has gotten out of control, D'Angelo."

I nodded in agreement.

"You have to be careful," he continued. "You have to be careful with the people you surround yourself with, not everybody is destined to be your friend, not everybody is destined to be your friend forever. Some people are in your life for a season, some are for a reason. If you hold on to those who are only supposed to be in your life for a season, they'll definitely give you a reason to let them go. That doesn't mean they're bad people, it just means you are in two different seasons."

In an instant, our innocent greeting and conversation evolved into a deep and meaningful lecture. I was intrigued, his tone and message flowed like spoken word poetry. It felt as if I was talking to my grandpa. I never got a chance to meet my grandpa as he passed away before I was born. I assumed if I ever were to talk to my grandpa, it would be something like this.

"And then you have people who are just plain evil," he continued.

"Yes sir" I agreed, nodding my head.

"They are the people who wish you harm, and actually do harm, and you know what you do with those people?" he asked while leaning closer.

"Hm?"

"You can do two things with those people. "One: Don't associate with them. If you give evil people enough space and time, they'll damn themselves. They'll be consumed by the same fire that they have created-"

I didn't move a muscle as I continued to listen on as if I was a child listening to a ghost story before bed. I remained silent, as I didn't dare intervene with his thought process. Despite his smooth demeanor, he spoke with great passion and urgency.

"You can't always avoid them, but if you can, steer clear away. If you can't, the only other option is to fight fire with water."

I squinted my eyes and tilted my head after hearing those words. I wasn't sure where he was leading with his point or what exactly made him pick this topic. I know some elderly people just like to have someone to talk to and be heard. His words were interesting and insightful nonetheless.

"Yup", he reaffirmed. "Because think about it, are you going to fight evil with evil? Fire with fire? Or violence with violence? That's what they want you to do!"

I leaned back in my seat and took a deep breath, internalizing the advice he was giving me.

"You heard about the youngin not too far from here? Gutted! in his own house?"

"Yeah, I did."

"I pray for them, that was a terrible thing that happened, but that's the kind of thing people want vengeance for, that's the devil working on both ends."

"You have to be strong enough to break the cycle," I added.

He leaned over eagerly and pointed his finger to me.

"And that's why you are highly favored boy!" he said with a big smile. He raised his hand in the air, and we gave each other a high five. His face lit up as if he struck gold.

"See? I don't have to worry about you. Your mom and grandma are so proud of you- I'm proud of you. You're going to do great things D'Angelo."

Hearing those words sent chills up my spine, and gave me goosebumps. I was nearly overwhelmed with the positive energy and reassurance he instilled in me at that moment. Most of those positive words are the same thing my mom and grandma used to tell me growing up, and they used to make me feel good as well, but this time the message struck me a little differently, and actually reached me to my core. I don't know if it is because of the mental state I was in at the moment and I was in dire need of cheerful words, or possibly because I've received the message from a stranger, maybe both.

"Thank you very much sir! I appreciate that."

He reached over and gave me a firm handshake.

"Of course D'Angelo."

I felt my cell phone vibrate in my left pocket. I quickly checked and saw a text message from Milly.

I'll be there in a couple of hours, she wrote with a heart emoji.

I totally forgot, she was coming over that afternoon to hang out and have pizza tonight. I rolled my eyes in annoyance.

"Yeah, I have to go but it was great meeting you- again!" I said while standing up.

Using the back of the church bench in front of him he hoisted himself up and slowly turned around to meet me face to face and gave me another firm handshake.

"D'Angelo! It's been a pleasure!"

"Oh and what is your name again?" I asked as I backed my way out between the church benches.

"Theodore," he replied.

"Theodore! Awesome, I'll see you around."

"Give my best to your family!"

As I entered the red carpet aisle, I waved goodbye but before I was able to turn my back to walk away, he called for me.

"Oh and D'Angelo! Don't forget to-" he then pointed up the aisle and began to do the sign of the cross.

Understanding what he meant, I smiled and nodded in agreement, and hastily made my way up the aisle. I looked down at the holy water stoup made of stone, dipped my fingers, and began to cross myself once more. I turned to walk out of the church but paused before exiting, as something drew my curiosity back to the holy water stoup. I slowly stepped over and grabbed the cool and rugged edge of the stoup with both my hands. I looked down and saw my murky reflection in the holy water.

Chapter
TWELVE

JUDGEMENT

Later that day, I sat on my bed surrounded by print-ed documents with yellow highlighted sections while reading my notes from my journalism class. The class was focused heavily on terminology, so most of my studying relied on photographic memory. Not only was I preparing for an exam the following week, I had to submit a response for one of the documents Professor Joseph emailed for us to read. It was a usual day at the proverbial office for me, besides the fact that Milly was a mere few feet away from me obsessing over her image in the mirror.

Milly stood in front of the mirror playing with her hair, admiring herself. Milly never put much effort in her looks as she was naturally cute. She didn't wear much makeup or jewelry, nor would she be considered a 'fashionista', but today was different. She wore eyeliner and her hair shimmered in the light as it seemed freshly done and curled. Unlike to her usual loose and comfortable attire, she wore a fitted dark red V-neck shirt that laid snug against her breast. A silver chain necklace hung around her neck with a black heart pendant sitting just above her cleavage. Her fitted dark blue jeans complemented her figure as she twitched back and forth anxiously side to side. Overall she looked hot so I wasn't complaining, but this was definitely odd of Milly as we have no plans of going out today.

My eyes would wander from my notebook to Milly, not only because I was enjoying what I was seeing, but because my gut instincts were reminding me that Milly was still possessed. I'm sure she caught my gaze from the reflection of the mirror. To the naked eye she seemed like a normal, attractive young latina, but I wasn't fooled.

"Ugh!" Milly barked, "how much longer do you have to study?"

I almost forgot Milly said she had something to show me when she first came over. I

honestly wasn't in the mood for any drama or theatrics. I was apprehensive about allowing her over in the first place, especially since we made little to no progress in getting whatever demon or curse out of Milly. I was hoping to have a normal meet up as we usually did on Fridays.

"I don't know, maybe another hour," I answered.

"I want to show you a trick I've been working on!"

"A trick? You don't need any other tricks, you can walk on walls and ceilings,

you're a demon from hell, I get it." I pointed to the spot above my door frame where the handprints and claw marks still remained. I was able to scrub off some of the prints and markings that were on the ceiling above my bed a couple of days ago. I eventually gave up because of the amount of scrubbing I had to do to just clean a couple of them off. It was good enough for me for the time being.

She rolled her eyes in the mirror and turned to face me.

"That was like a week ago, get over it."

I wasn't sure what was more shocking to me; her new snappy attitude, or the fact that she

believes one week is enough time to get over the fact that a demon inside of her crawled up my bedroom walls tracking claw prints.

"And I still can't get it out!" I argued.

"Shh! You're just bad at cleaning"

"Really?" I said incredulously.

"Look! I've been practicing this for a minute, you're going to love it!" She protested.

Realizing there's no avoiding what's to come I caved in and closed my notebook. Whatever she wanted to show me couldn't be that bad, or else she wouldn't have been so eager. Annoyed, I rolled my eyes and flicked my hand in the air, signaling her to proceed with her show and tell.

Like a stubborn child who gets her way at the end, she grinned from ear to ear and excitement radiated out of her body. She placed her feet together and stood with her shoulders back, and put her hands at her sides. She gave me one final look before closing her eyes and taking a bow. When she raised her torso to stand straight up again, her appearance changed in an instant. She was now a few inches taller with long jet-black hair with deep long curls. Her usual round face was now thin, as was her waist. She was no longer Milly, but she was now Jessica.

I sat completely still, my eyes locked forward. I tried desperately to

make sense of what I had just witnessed. I guess my reaction was the outcome Milly was looking for as she stood there with satisfaction written across her face.

"What the hell?" I asked.

"I know right? I look like that girl you have a crush on in your journalism class! I even

sound like her." Milly cleared her throat, correcting her vocal tone to match Jessica's. "I even sound like her, what's her name? Tess? Jess?"

"It's Jessica!" I said, correcting her. "And time out—"

"Not gonna lie D'Angelo, you have a type; curvy and curly haired girls?" she said as she

began petting her newly acquired locks.

Although embarrassing, Milly told no lies, but I couldn't give her the satisfaction of

being right, nor putting me in a box.

"Hey! I don't have a type, and you need to change back right now, this is getting kinda

creepy."

"No! Come on, you can practice talking to her like *this*, and maybe you can ask her out."

Milly locked eyes with me, dipping her chin and placing her hands behind her back. She then took a few steps towards me, slightly swaying her hips. Before I knew it, she was standing over me, looking down upon me with those beautiful light brown eyes that did not belong to her.

"Excuse me D'Angelo, would you like to study some time together?" she asked.

I forgot how to speak, it was all too surreal. I wanted to say 'hell yeah', but my brain and

motor functions were disconnected. Seduced? No. I was weak and powerless as she towered over me, staring into my soul.

"D'Angelo?" she continued.

I was admiring Jessica's beauty, how could she be even more beautiful standing before

me? It's not even really her—but somehow she's here, in my room, in Milly's body? What the actual fuck is going on?

A loud clapping sound snapped me out of my deep thoughts. As I awoke from my day

dream, Milly stood before me, appearing as her normal self again. She looked at me with wide eyes and her hands together, waiting to see if I had properly snapped out of my daze.

"I'm—sorry" I said.

"Yeah, you need a lot of practice." she suggested before turning away back to the mirror.

As she turned, I could see her giddy smile in the mirror, pleased by my innocent reaction.

At the thought of how helpless and lost I was in that brief moment, I couldn't hold back

from finding humor in it myself. Supernatural or not, we shared yet another classic moment of Milly and D'Angelo.

The day came to a close as the moon rose and the temperature plummeted, but our night was just beginning.

I SPENT THE REST OF THE DAY WITH MILLY CATCHING her up to speed with my research on demonology, exorcisms, and witchcraft. With all the talk about demons and the paranormal reminded me of Ricky and his family's grief. The impact Joshua's death had on Ricky's family was weighing on me. We haven't spoken about it and I thought it was important for her to know just how much damage had been done.

"Milly?" I said hesitantly, calling her attention.

"Yeah?"

"Do you happen to remember the guy you killed?"

Milly sighed as if she dreaded revisiting that topic, let alone that entire day.

"No not really, I try not to think too much about it," she said.

"Do you remember his face?"

"There was too much blood!" she snapped. "It was like a bad dream, and I woke up to a dead body covered in-"Milly paused, clearly bothered. "As soon as I saw the dead body I looked away, got dressed and left." A moment of silence passed. "Why?" she asked.

I swallowed the lump in my throat and my mouth became dry.

"Because it was Joshua," I answered.

Milly's eyes shifted to the side, trying to think.

"Who the hell is Joshua?" she asked, deeply confused.

"Ricky's cousin" I answered, hoping to connect the dots.

Milly gasped as her jaw dropped and grabbed the top of her head with both hands. "The dick head from the party?" she asked desperately.

I nodded.

"Oh shit, oh fuck, oh shit!" She said, pacing back and forth. "What? Why? How?"

I stood up from sitting on my bed. "Milly, if you don't know—I sure as hell don't."

"So that means—Ricky."

"Yes, Ricky, but not just Ricky, his entire family is in shambles."

Milly dropped her arms to her sides in defeat. Her eyes had become glassy and her lips started to quiver. She clenched her fists, likely trying to hold in her emotions. The same emotions she's been holding in for the past week as well I'm sure.

"Does—" Milly cleared her throat. "Does Ricky, um—"

"No, Ricky doesn't know. But he was a drunken mess when I saw him, but no."

It was then that we were finally on the same page. Denial and wishful thinking was no longer an option. The demonic spirit inside Milly was very much real and very dangerous. Stalling and lying to ourselves is only putting more innocent lives at risk, including our own. So I proposed an idea.

"I was thinking maybe we should go through and actually get an exorcism," I suggested.

Milly lightly tapped the corners of her eyes with her knuckles, drying them. Milly nodded her head vigorously, submitting to the idea.

We soon hopped on my computer and began searching for local places that could perform and exorcism. I could only find one in The Bronx, which had a hefty price tag, and even then he stated on his website that he needed to get the Bishop's approval. We agreed to go tomorrow after my Saturday class. We figured since this is an emergency, he'd likely do one without having to go to see a Bishop for permission.

With a plan set in motion, and cheesy pizza on the brain, it felt as if there was a light at the end of the tunnel for us. After some time, a delicate smile returned to Milly's face, which let me know she had felt the same.

I stood proudly in front of the mirror, as if I was a boss calling the shots. Milly sat on my bed watching me.

"Alright, I'ma go and get the pizza" I said as I threw on my lucky leather jacket. "Can you do me a favor and not open another portal to hell?"

"That was one time, and besides, this isn't the first time you left me alone in your house."

"No, this is the first time I'm letting '*possessed you*' stay over by yourself."

Milly scrunched her lip and looked to the floor.

"Point taken." she said.

"Exactly."

I walked towards my bedroom's backdoor, and placed my hand on the doorknob.

"The front door is locked, and I'm leaving out the back door so I don't wake my grandma, okay?"

"Okay, I'll take a nap till you get back," she said, snatching off her shoes.

"Perfect," I responded as I unlocked the door. I pulled open my door and was met with the crisp air that flowed through my apartment building's hallway.

I would go and get our pizza pie, and come back. It all sounded well and simple, a little too simple, so much so a gut feeling told me I had to reiterate myself and make my point clear to Milly. Before stepping outside, I looked back at Milly who was a mere moments away from getting completely comfortable and resting her head on my pillow.

"Milly?" I called.

With innocent eyes, she looked up at me from the other side of my bookcase headboard.

"—No portals!" I finished.

"Got it" she said, rolling her eyes.

With a subtle nod of approval, I turned away and stepped out into the hallway, closing the door behind me. For a moment I believe to have been overreacting with Milly, she couldn't do anything in there by herself. And even if she wanted to do something, I'm just going to the store, fifteen minute trip? Twenty tops? What could she do in that amount of time? I trust her.

After locking the door, I descended down the staircase eagerly. It's about 9PM, and the Pizza place closes at 10PM. Luckily I lived just a couple of blocks away, so I don't have to worry too much about getting there before it closes. I just hate being one of the last customers, I know the employees are tired and want to go home, I know I would.

Exiting out of my building, the night life in my neighborhood seemed to be going without a hitch. Some guys drinking off to the side of my building, some people playing music across the street from a small speaker while smoking hookah. Some cars were double parked making traffic on the street a bitch. One of them being a black van that slightly towered over the rest.

After a short walk, I made it to the pizzeria and stood at the window counter outside. The store owner Gustavo, a tall elderly man who knew me since I was a little boy, saw me leaning on the counter waiting. He greeted me with a big smile and swung his arms wide open.

"D'Angelo! How are you doing?" he said, giving me a high five.

"I'm doing good and you?"

"That's good, I'm well thanks! What can I get for you today?"

"That's good, I'll have a small pie, half sausage, half pineapple"

I'm not taking any responsibility for the pineapple, that's all Milly.

"We're out of pineapple, I'm sorry" he said.

"Oh okay, pepperoni would do fine thanks!"

"You got it," he said joyfully, giving me a thumbs-up.

He walked back towards the oven and wiped his hands on a white rag that stuck out of his apron pocket.

I turned my back to the pizzeria window and took a deep breath, enjoying the refreshing cool air topped with a pizza aroma. The neighborhood seemed busy again, kids running up and down the street, and the stores were full of customers doing last minute shopping for the weekend. The fear on people's faces seemed to have faded away, and the terror that happened last week with Joshua was old news. In that moment of peace, I was utterly thankful.

A police car blaring its sirens at the end of the block caught my attention. I watched it as it drove down the block under the train tracks, hastily in my direction. I stood still, trying to not look suspicious or guilty for that matter. The police car continued past me and began to turn left onto my block where I lived. My heart dropped, causing me to lose my calm and cool composure. I stepped away from the pizzeria, and locked my focus on the police car.

With my apartment building in the not so far distance, I watched the police car intensely

as it approached. My leg began to twitch anxiously, praying that it did not stop in front of my building. As the police car crept behind the black van, I took a step forward, ready to bolt down the street. Just as I was about to lunge forward, the police car swerved around the parked black van and continued its way past my building. My nerves began to ease as the police car faded in the distance along with its loud siren.

I checked my surroundings, looking to see if anybody noticed my distraught look, but people instead walked past me, paying me no attention. To be sure, I reached in my pocket and pulled out my phone. No missed calls, and no text messages from Milly—thank God.

"Hey D'Angelo!" yelled Gustavo, startling me. He stood there at the pizzeria window holding a pizza box open, with my pizza pie inside. "Do you want any seasoning?" he asked.

"No thank you!" I said, tucking my phone away back in my pocket.

He nodded his head and placed the pizza box on the counter and began to tie it close. I walked up to the counter taking out my wallet, as he stuffed a small stack of napkins under the pizza box string. After I paid him, he gave me another firm handshake.

"Thank you so much," he said.

"Thank you!" I said while walking away.

As I walked home with a pep in my step, I was overjoyed at the thought of sharing another fun Friday pizza night with Milly. I began to think of it as a night of celebration, with our new found light at the end of the tunnel, a priest that could help us. Finally, we can put this all behind us.

Short of breath, I eventually made it back to my bedroom back door. As I unlocked and opened the door, I was reminded that I couldn't get the pineapple toppings on her pizza, and figured I would break the news as soon as I saw her.

"Hey Milly, they didn't have pineapple, so I got you—" I paused immediately, horrified at the scene in my room.

At first glance walking in, Milly stood in the center of my bedroom hunched over with her back turned to me. At her feet lay a bloodbath of two victims; one was a man in a leather jacket and cargo jeans and tactical boots, lying face down in a pool of his own blood. The other was a woman propped against my dresser facing me, in a similar attire. Her head tilted to the side, exposing the giant chunk of flesh ripped out of her neck. Blood continued to pour out of her wound in a steady gentle stream, flowing down her jacket and encapsulating her legs and hands on the floor. It looked as if two people were trapped in the room with a tiger, and I was next.

"—pepperoni," I muttered.

Turning my attention to Milly, I stood in place, not wanting to move a muscle, petrified that the slightest movement would set her off to attack me next. Possessed or not, I believed Milly was still in there, somewhere. I thought that maybe the sound of my voice would bring her to her right state of mind.

"Milly, what the hell happened?" I asked.

Her head and shoulders twitched, before slowly turning to face me. It was only then I saw Milly at her absolute worst state yet. With her head tilted forward, hair in a curly mess, she stared at me with hateful blood thirsty red demonic eyes. Black and purple veins traced the left side of her face. The lower half of her face was smeared with the blood of her victims as well as her chest and hands. The tip of her pearly fangs peered just over her crimson lips.

I had accepted the fact that I was but a lamb ready for slaughter, in the center of my own room, struck down and mangled by my best friend. Looking deep into her eyes, Milly was nowhere to be found, only a rabid demonic animal ready to kill.

Without so much as blinking, she took a step forward, sending a shock wave throughout my body, awakening me from my petrified state.

"Milly, please!" I begged.

Those words only seemed to have angered her, causing one of her eyes to twitch and snarl her upper lip. Her next two footsteps would send pulses of fear that would radiate up my leg, making me weak at the knees.

In a split second, I remembered I'm not completely defenseless. I had an ace up my sleeve. Theodore's words crept into my head; *The only other option is to fight fire with water.* I dropped the pizza box and hastily snatched the spray bottle I had on the dresser to my left. Without hesitation, I pointed it at Milly and gave one firm spray like my life depended on it, which it did.

Milly threw her head back in anguish, letting out a moan. A disembodied hiss echoed in my room. Milly groaned in pain covering her face with the palms of her hands. Steam arose from her, like a pot of boiling water. The toxic stench of burning flesh and brimstone radiated off of her, flooding my nose.

I stood back and waited to see how much damage I had done.

After a moment, Milly stood still, cupping her face with her hands, regaining her composure, taking deep slow breaths. She threw her hands down violently, and looked at me intensely.

I leaned in with amazement, noticing her eyes and face were back to normal. I felt a tiny sense of relief, but the expression on her face let me know I wasn't completely out of the woods just yet.

"What the hell was that?!" Milly asked.

"It was holy water!"

"Why do you have holy water, knowing I'm possessed by a damn demon?"

"I have it *because* you're possessed by a damn demon."

"I was joking! That shit burns!"

"Oh yeah, I can tell you was joking with the girl with her throat ripped out in my bedroom!"

"They were trying to kill me!"

"What the hell do you mean they were trying to kill you? Who are they? How did they get in here?"

"I don't know! I didn't ask them."

My eyes wandered past Milly and observed the massacre. Seeing the two lifeless bodies and blood all over the rug, floor and furniture, reality had sunk in. My bedroom was now a crime scene.

"Oh my God, Milly—what the hell are we going to do? What am I supposed to tell my grandma?"

"She's blind, you're good."

I balled my fists. A fire burned inside of me and a voice was clawing its way out, desperately wanting to show a side of me she has never seen. Her nonchalant ways had me ready to explode, and so I was.

"Milly! Are you—"

A loud boom erupted behind me, knocking me out of my infuriated state, startling me and Milly. From the corner of my eye, I saw my back door swing wide open. I took a step aside, and stood beside Milly anxious to see what the hell was next, but nothing could prepare me for what I was about to see.

Gun in hand, the intruder marched in with authority and stood in front of us. The intruder swayed their aim back and forth between Milly and I.

"Alright you two, stay right where you are, and put your hands where—" Locking eyes with me, the intruder's face went pale. "D'Angelo?"

Milly and I looked at each other, and from the expression on her face, she was as flabbergasted as I was. Goosebumps ran across my body as I tried desperately to believe what I was seeing. Frozen, I could only mutter her name.

"Jessica?"

Chapter
THIRTEEN

THE HIGH PRIESTESS

My bedroom stood quiet and motionless, while a war of emotions took place in my mind. Fear rumbled in the pit of my stomach, I was reluctant to move a muscle. With my throat in knots, I was begging for someone, anyone, to say something and break this silence yet only our eyes spoke.

Jessica didn't shift her focus from me, standing petrified as if she were ashamed of herself and caught in the act. With her aim still in Milly's direction, her shoulders began to relax as did the tension in her elbows.

As Jessica gradually lowered the gun, it became easier to breathe, and the knots in my throat loosened. Just as I was prepared to speak, Jessica's head snapped forward to Milly's direction with fierce eyes full of disdain. Her arms shot straight forward with Milly's forehead just inches away from the barrel of the gun.

"D'Angelo talk! What the hell are you doing here?"

"This is my bedroom!"

Milly looked over at me with glassy eyes, pleading for me to do something. We both knew if anybody was going to be shot it would be her. Being covered in blood with two dead people behind her didn't put her in a positive light.

"You remember Milly, right?" I continued.

"Yeah, Ricky's birthday party," she mumbled.

"Yeah, she's—"

"She's the fucking demon we've been looking for!" Jessica said while rattling the gun in Milly's direction causing her to flinch. "She killed Joshua Bautista!"

"Jessica! Listen to me, it's not what it looks like—"

"It looks like she just killed two of my men."

"They were trying to kill me!" Milly interjected.

"Yeah, no shit!" Jessica snapped.

"You're not helping," I told Milly.

Turning my attention back to Jessica, I spoke in a soft and calm voice as if I was negotiating with a hostage taker.

"Jessica, we need your help, Milly is possessed, obviously, but we're working on getting that fixed."

"D'Angelo, it's not that simple," she spoke hastily. "You've been harboring a killer demon—"

"But she's not a killer demon!" I paused. "She's *possessed* by one!"

Jessica turned her face to me with squinted eyes and a snarled lip.

"I just need time to explain," I continued.

A slushy gurgling sound turned our attention to Milly, who was fixated on the palms of her hands. We all watched along as the blood smeared across Milly's skin began to soak into her body, eventually disappearing altogether. Only the dark spots of blood staining the collar of her shirt remained. We looked at each other confused, hoping we all just witnessed the same thing.

As Jessica stood teetering back and forth examining Milly in disbelief, the sound of a walkie-talkie muffled from her leather jacket pocket. Jessica remained still in deep thought, lowering her gun even more. Her anxious eyes vibrated as they twitched between where Milly and I stood. Her erratic eyes and racing mind came to a screeching halt.

"D'Angelo, is there anybody else in the house?" she asked.

"Just my Grandma, she's blind and she in her bedroom, in the back"

"Okay—"

The walkie-talkie sounded off again in her pocket. "Jess, do you hear me? Over."

Jessica, rolling her eyes, snatched the walkie-talkie out of her hand. Before talking into the radio, she placed her index finger to her lips, signaling for both of us to be quiet.

"I'm in, clearing each room, standby, over." Jessica dropped her arm holding the walkie-talkie and turned her attention to me. "D, we have 60 seconds, are you good friends with any of your neighbors so you can stay there?"

On a dime, me and Milly looked at each other as we both knew the answer.

"Yeah, Carla, across the hall."

"Perfect, let's go!"

Jessica swiftly turned around and headed out the back door as Milly and I followed closely behind her. As we exited my bedroom and into the hallway, Jessica turned back to me and grabbed my shoulder.

"Which apartment? Are they home?"

"Right there, apartment 3E" I pointed out. "She should be home."

Jessica led the charge to Carla's door and hastily knocked. Me and Milly joined her at her sides, patiently waiting to take orders from Jessica. The smell of weed seeped from under the door.

The door swung open and the aroma hit us like a tidal wave. Carla stood in the doorway alarmed, wearing an oversized gray shirt.

"Hey, what happened?" Carla asked with confusion.

"No time!" Jessica said, cutting her off. Jessica placed one foot inside and held the door wide open with her arm. She stepped aside, making space for me and Milly to walk through.

"Carla is it?" she asked sharply.

Carla nodded with wide eyes. "Great, D'Angelo and Milly need to stay here." Jessica said, pushing us inside. "And everybody needs to be quiet, do you understand me?"

"Wait! What the hell is happening?" Carla asked.

"D'Angelo, will explain—briefly!" Jessica said, gritting her teeth.

Jessica's piercing eyes told me everything of what I should and should not say, striking fear into my bloodstream like a strict parent telling their child to behave or else suffer the consequences.

"D'Angelo—I'll text you when it's safe, do not leave or make too much noise, for the love of god!" she said desperately.

We all agreed, looking at one another.

The walkie-talkie, in her hand made a beeping sound, alerting the whole room. "Jess status update, over."

Jessica hushed us all again before she took a deep breath and regained her composure. She then placed the walkie-talkie in her mouth.

"I got two personnel down, I need back up and a clean up crew, target is lost, I repeat, target is lost." Jessica pulled the doorknob shut behind her.

A moment of silence passes. Carla slowly turns around to face me.

"What the fuck is happening?"

I figured Jessica wanted me to keep the whole demon and murdering stuff a secret, so I had to get creative, but more importantly, convincing.

"Uh- my friend Jessica is a cop and they're patrolling the building for a—killer."

"A killer?" she asked, sounding terrified. "Who? Who did they kill? Why couldn't you just go to your own apartment?"

Milly curled her lips in and raised her eyebrows, as if she knew I was screwed coming up with another logical lie. A moment passed as Carla grew impatient, rattling her head and looking deep into my eyes. At that moment I thought of a clever way to take the attention and heat off of me.

"Well I forgot my keys, and Milly actually saved someone after the killer sliced them— with a knife!" Milly looked at me, deeply surprised and confused as to why I threw her in my reckless alibi, yet it worked apparently.

"Oh my god! Are you okay?" she asked Milly, grabbing her hand.

Unsure of what to say, Milly just smiled and nodded, but before I was in the clear, a few blood stains on Milly's shirt caught my eye. I decided it was best for me to point them out before Carla did.

"Yeah and that's why she has the blood on her shirt!" I added with urgency.

Carla's jaw dropped as she gasped at the sight of Milly's shirt. She took a step to Milly, closing the gap and eliminating any personal space. It wasn't long before Carla turned her attention from Milly's cleavage to her eyes. A smirk slithered its way onto her face, as she was clearly basking in the moment.

I still wasn't too sure on how to feel at the sight of Carla and Milly staring into each other's eyes. Part of me was turned on, while the other part of me felt like a third wheel. Overall I was relieved that I was able to distract Carla momentarily and get her mind off of asking too many questions.

A flurry of knocks hit the front door, snapping Carla and Milly from their intimate moment. I figured it had to be Jessica, so I rushed past them, opening the door expeditiously. A pizza box rushed in and landed in my arms.

"Shh!" Jessica hissed, quickly slamming the door.

I was so scared and overwhelmed that I had totally forgotten that I had a whole pizza pie in my room! I looked back at Milly and Carla as if I struck gold, entirely thankful because I was becoming extremely hungry. Thanks to Jessica, we won't have to go the rest of the night hungry as we hid away.

"She is the best!" I whispered.

A bustle of footsteps erupted on the other side of the door, silencing me and cutting my celebration short. I signaled for Milly and Carla to remain silent as I pressed my ear against the door to listen.

I could only hear a flurry of footsteps and hushed murmurs filling the hallway. There must have been at least ten, maybe fifteen people scurrying on the other side of the door. I sat waiting intensely, in hopes of picking up any information or even just Jessica's voice. The murmuring voices and scuffling footsteps faded away into silence.

I stood up and held my breath as I looked through the peephole. No movement or sound came from the hallway, only dead silence. An all black figure walked in front of the peephole, startling me, making my knees buckle. I covered my mouth and nose with my hand, blocking any air to come in or out of my body. As I remained crouched, perfectly still, I noticed the shadow of the man on the other side, creeping its way in from under the door. I stared down at the black mass, waiting desperately for it to pass. After a brief standstill, the shadow moved out of sight, followed by the sound of heavy footsteps fading away, allowing me to finally breathe.

I peered back at Milly and Carla who stood together looking at me with wide eyes, anxiously waiting. With the coast clear, I stood up and walked over to the couch in Carla's living room and took a seat, placing the pizza box to my side.

"Are we good?" Milly whispered.

"Yeah I think so."

"You guys aren't the killer so why are you hiding?" Carla questioned.

"We don't need to be questioned by detectives, they'll pull witnesses. Including you Gabs," I answered.

"Oh."

Milly walked over and took a seat on the other side of the pizza box. I grabbed the string tied around the pizza box with both fists and cut it by pressing down with my thumb.

"Here, have some pizza" I offered Carla as I discarded the broken string.

As Carla inched her way over to us, I opened the pizza box and was welcomed to a cheesy golden delight with pepperoni and sausage. The pie looked extra delicious as the grease glistened under the soft light filtering through the window.

"It's in perfect condition! Still kinda warm too!" I announced.

"Yes! I'm hungry," Milly said.

"Aren't you already full?" I joked, causing Milly to laugh sarcastically. I looked up at Carla and saw the confused expression written across her face. "It's an inside joke Carla, don't worry."

"Ahh," Carla said.

I placed the pizza box on the glass table in front of me, sliding it beside Carla's ashtray that still had a lit marijuana cigarette in it. I figured if anybody was to have the first slice, it should be Carla as she was probably experiencing the munchies already. That, and the unwelcome intrusion into her home.

"Here, you can have the first slice, pepperoni or sausage?"

Without much thought, she reached down and pulled herself a slice of pepperoni pizza, followed by Milly.

"Thank you!" she said while chewing.

"It's no problem, it's the least we can do after barging in." I peeled off a slice of pizza with sausage topping.

Carla let out a muffled "Mmm", with her mouth full. After some more chewing she continued. "I have some paper plates." Carla then walked off to her kitchen and returned with a stack of paper plates, passing one to both Milly and I.

With our mouths full, Milly and I looked at each other, smiling with puckered greasy lips. As crazy and hectic this pizza night was, we clearly knew that this one particular night was one for the books.

One slice turned into two slices as did one hour became several. We enjoyed each other's company, keeping each other entertained with small talk and sharing nostalgic memories of growing up in the neighborhood. No matter how much we enjoyed the moment, we made sure to not cause too much noise in fear that the people out in the hallway would hear us.

It was 2AM and I had begun to worry, spiraling in my own thoughts, so much so that Milly noticed it in my face. When Carla stepped away to grab something from her bedroom, Milly saw an opportunity to ask.

"D, what's wrong?" she whispered.

"A lot Milly, I don't know what's gonna happen! I haven't heard anything out there and I haven't received any text from Jessica either."

"Okay give it time, obviously she's gonna help us."

"Yeah, but what the fuck is she? I have never seen her like that, now she's some kind of—demonic vigilante?"

"Maybe, either way she's a badass."

I couldn't help but agree, but the image of Jessica marching into my bedroom with her gun drawn replayed in my head over and over. I couldn't believe this beautiful girly-girl could go from taking college classes during the day, and apparently doing whatever 'this' is at night.

After having a third slice of cold pizza, and vocalizing my concerns with Milly some more, I began to lean back and relax on the couch. I locked my gaze at the window, fixated on the dark night sky, with colorful and bright glistening lights on the low horizon. My eyelids grew heavy, and the bustling sounds of the city lulled me to sleep.

SEVERAL HOURS LATER I WOKE UP WITH MY HEAD RESTing on the arm of the couch with a dull hazy beam of sunlight hitting my face. My morning was welcomed with Milly's legs draped over mine as she laid nearly completely flat on her back, and her head resting on the opposite end of the couch. I closed my eyes again, still exhausted from the night before. I was so tired, I almost forgot what made me worn out in the first place. My phone's alarm began to ring, but I was still so sleepy I was able to turn it off without having to open my eyes. It wasn't until the thought of my grandma crossed my mind, that I had remembered everything, jolting me from the couch.

I began to push myself off the couch, fighting the urge to lay back down. I sporadically reached my right hand out to my sides, grasping at the air, desperately trying to find something to hold onto. I clawed at the floor, pulling myself off, eventually causing Milly's legs to slide off and me ending up on the floor. I took a deep breath and stretched my eyes open. I don't know if Carla's couch was just comfortable as hell or I was just over tired from the chaotic night, probably both. I only had a few hours of sleep anyways.

I struggled to stand up straight, staggering in place like a drunk person. I let out a yawn and shook my head to fully wake myself up, shaking off the drowsiness.

Milly began to shift around on the couch, just before her eyes gently opened, glistening with joy.

"What's up?" she said grinning.

"My blood pressure," I responded while stretching.

From the backroom, Carla emerged, walking in the living room with a cup of coffee in hand. "Good morning you two." She seemed to have been well rested.

"Good morning," Milly and I said in unison.

Milly sat up from the couch and turned to face me. "What time is it?" she asked with squinted eyes.

I slid my phone out from my pants pocket. "It's 8:15 AM" I said.

"Did you get a text from that girl?" Carla asked.

I checked my phone once more. "No," I responded, sounding disappointed.

We exchanged looks to one another for a moment. Not a word was said, but I can tell we were all worried about what to do.

"You think something happened to her?" I continued.

"Uh... I don't think so," Milly answered.

Carla stepped forward hastily. "You think the killer is still out there?"

"What killer?" I asked.

"The killer from last night, remember?"

"Oh yeah! The killer! Um- nah I'm sure they got em." You have to cut me some slack, I had just woken up and forgot the lies I had to scramble together.

My mind began to shuffle, thinking of scenarios and options of what to do now that possibly Jessica had left us high and dry. I had to leave for class soon, and besides we couldn't stay in Carla's forever.

Just as I dropped my arms to my sides, my phone vibrated in my hand. I snatched my phone up to my face eagerly to see what I was notified about. The heavens opened up and the air began to clear.

"I got a text from her!" I said with joy.

Carla took a sip of her coffee and gently placed it on the coffee table. Milly adjusted herself as she leaned forward, ready for what I was about to read. Both looked thrilled and overjoyed.

I read aloud, "Good Morning D'Angelo, it's safe to go back to your apartment, but only you and Milly please."

"That's it?" Milly said. "No update on the situation?"

"Yeah, did they catch the killer?" Carla added. "Where is she?"

"I don't know that's all she said."

Milly and Carla exchanged a look to one another, both seeming equally annoyed. I was too, to be honest. Although we were in the clear, we were still in the dark. But there was no time to waste and sulk.

"Okay she said it's safe for me to go back to our apartment, so I'll just ring the doorbell and have my grandma let me in" I stated. "Carla, you stay here, and if you go out, be careful." I figured stating what we should do would make us all feel a bit better, giving us some sort of direction to focus on. A small plan of action is better than no plan of action.

Carla chugged some of her coffee. "You got it! And I'll watch the news, just in case they say something about the killer."

"You do that!" I said sharply. Although I highly doubt a news reporter was going to be in my bedroom covering a story of a demon killing two people. But hey, Carla was distracted and out of the way.

"Milly, come with me" I ordered.

Milly stood up eagerly, and followed me to the front door. As I reached out for the doorknob, I hesitated and gave one last look to Milly, checking to see if she was ready. I was unsure of what to expect stepping outside, yet Milly stood there, grinning deviously like she was enjoying the thrill of it all.

I unlocked the door and steadily opened it wide. Apart from the rumbling sound of a train in the distance, the hallway remained silent. I stood still, anticipating for something to emerge from our blind spots, but only a blank white wall stood opposite of the door.

Like crossing a two way street, I looked both ways before stepping out into the hallway. The coast was clear, so I signaled for Milly to step out and follow me. Hunched over, she closed the door gently behind her. I made an effort to not look suspicious just in case with my back straight and nearly every muscle clenched as I made my way to my apartment front door. If someone were to be watching us, we would definitely seem as if we had something to hide.

I took out my keys and opened the front door apprehensively. The front door made an eerie creaking sound as

I opened it. I looked in both directions and noticed that all the lights were off in the apartment, even in my bedroom. A cheerful voice down the foyer in the kitchen startled me.

"Is that my D'Angelo?"

"Yeah—yeah? Grandma?" I said.

"We're in the kitchen!"

I was relieved to know my grandma was okay but was a little thrown off from hearing the word 'we'. I looked back at Milly to see if she heard the same as I had and she seemed equally confused. I marched my way to the kitchen to investigate, but I wasn't prepared to see Jessica, sitting with my grandma at the kitchen table.

Chapter
FOURTEEN

THREE OF PENTACLES

The sight of Jessica sitting with my grandma rocked me to my core, unaware she was even here. Jessica lowered a mug from her face after taking a sip, and greeted me with an innocent smile. Her thick lustrous and curly hair draped down her shoulders like 2 waterfalls. The sunlight gently beamed through the window, creating a soft glowing outline around her, making her look holy, pure, or godsent, but I wasn't fooled.

"Hey D'Angelo!" she said, "I told you he'd be back" she said to my grandma.

My grandma, in her pink butterfly pajamas, placed her mug down and eagerly swiveled in her wooden chair to turn and face me.

"D'Angelo! How come you never told me about the study group you invited over last night?" she asked.

"I—I um—"

"You have to give me a warning, I was scared out of my mind and you left?"

"Yeah well-"

"Oh my god! Thank goodness Jessica was here! She's a sweetheart, but still!"

"Yeah I'm sorry grandma, I was really busy running back and forth, and I had to um—" I couldn't complete the lie. I got nervous and before I knew it, I had pinned myself in a corner. I looked over to Jessica for help.

"He went over to Carla's place to print something right?"

"Yes! That's right" I agreed.

"Yeah but D'Angelo got so tired from working so hard, he took a nap over at Carla's house" Jessica said in a teasing playful tone.

"That's my grandson!" said my grandma cheerfully. "D'Angelo, why did you never introduce me to Jessica?"

"It's complicated—" I said.

"I remember you mentioning the name Jessica? Is this the one you danced with?"

Jessica snapped her head to me and blushed.

"Yes—" I said, gritting my teeth.

"Oh then she's a doll, she's in college, she can dance, has a good head on her shoulders." My grandma took a quick sip of her coffee. The moment she took to take a sip of her coffee made it seem like her rant was over, but she wasn't quite done yet. "I already like her more than Milly," she mumbled, followed by a chuckle.

Milly's jaw dropped and her eyes widened like an owl. I knew my Grandma was only kidding, but the joke didn't register well with Milly, as it caught Jessica off guard as well. Milly took a small step back, hiding behind the wall to the kitchen. Deep down, I knew Milly took it as a joke, even if there was a hint of hurtful truth behind it.

"Grandma, Milly is here," I said.

"Oop! I'm sorry Milly, you know I'm only kidding."

Milly took a step forward and peeked her forehead from around the corner of the kitchen entrance.

"Yeah, I know," Milly said with a monotone depressed voice.

"Okay, I think it's time me and D'Angelo discuss some things before heading off to school" Jessica said. She stood up from her seat and placed the mug in the sink. "It's been a pleasure talking to you Alice"

"The pleasure's all mine sweetheart, you all have a good day at school."

Jessica walked past me smiling, and made her way to my room. I looked back at Milly and noticed her eyes giving daggers to the back of Jessica's head. The evil predatory eyes had me convinced Milly was going to lunge and attack Jessica right then and there, but thankfully she restrained herself and instead followed me to my room.

As I walked into my bedroom, I was amazed at how neat and clean it was. There were no blood stains on my rug, floor or dresser. My bed was neatly made, and my pillows looked extra full and fluffy. I remembered the mess that the demon inside of Milly originally made on the top of my door frame and ceiling, and caused me to double check it. I could believe everything was spotless as if neither a demon or a double murder ever happened in here.

"Close the door," Jessica whispered.

Milly didn't budge her gaze from Jessica, nor did she make an attempt to close the door, so I hastily reached my arm behind her and closed the bedroom door myself.

"Both of you, sit"

"Don't bark orders at me," Milly said firmly.

Jessica noticeably became infuriated at Milly's back talk, with her snarled lip and piercing eyes.

"Milly, she saved our asses, just do what she says for now" I said, grabbing her shoulder. As I sat on my bed I pulled Milly down by her arm to sit next to me on my bed. She joined me, while crossing her legs and arms, rolling her eyes. Jessica looked down at us both like we were two criminals awaiting sentencing.

"Okay I want you both to understand something." She paused. "I am not only risking my job, but I'm risking my life for not eliminating you from the jump" she said while pointing at Milly. "We don't have much time, I need you to tell me what the hell is going on."

Milly unfolded her arms and legs and stood up straight, fixing her posture. "Well it all started last week—"

"Not you, D'Angelo," Jessica said.

At that moment, it not only felt as if I was in an interrogation room, but I was also being interrogated with an audience watching me. I'm kinda used to feeling a little nervous around Jessica, but this wasn't the kind of nerves you get when talking to a pretty girl. This is the kind of nerves you get when you feel as if your life depends on it, and if you say something wrong, the cards will fall.

After taking a deep breath in, I explained to Jessica what has happened the past week. Despite not knowing what Jessica could do, she might have been the only person who could really help us. With that in mind, I left no stone unturned when it came to recounting how hectic it has been for us. The deeper I explained in detail, the more weight it felt like was being lifted off of my shoulders, as this was the first time I was actually able to tell someone what was really happening. In a sense it was therapeutic to share and not feel like I was alone fighting this battle. I told Jessica everything, from Madam Maria, to Joshua and Ricky, even the exorcist we found on the internet.

In the midst of recounting the events from the past week, I noticed that the weight that was being taken off of my shoulders, was subtly being placed onto Jessica's. Her face became less tense, and her eyes looked heavy and glassy. By the time I got up to the part where I walked into my bedroom last night, she was pacing back and forth in front of us.

"So yeah we were actually going to go see the exorcist after school," I finished.

"That's bullshit!" Jessica snapped.

"How is that bullshit?"

"I know who you're talking about, you're talking about the guy in Riverdale, he's bullshit, we had to save his ass a few times, dealing with shit he's not supposed to!"

"So what do you suggest? We gotta do something"

Jessica continued to pace back and forth, biting her nails. I have never seen Jessica so stressed out before. I gave her a minute to think of what we could possibly do. I was reluctant to disturb Jessica's marching as that might only cause her to blow her top, but that didn't stop Milly.

"So you got any ideas or not?" Milly said.

Jessica quickly halted and turned around, giving Milly a look of disgust. "Do you have any idea of what you're dealing with? This witch, Madam Maria, has been abducting people and literally possessing them with demons and spirits for the past few months. We've been looking all over for her and we finally caught up with her apparently the same night you've been possessed."

"So there's other people like Milly!" I called out. "So what have you done to help those people?"

"We've shot them in the head, or cut their heads off."

"Oh" I said. I wasn't necessarily looking for that answer, nor was I expecting it. The image of Milly having her head cut off rattled me. My tongue grew stiff and my brain slightly dazed. "Wh—why can't you just do an exorcism then or something?"

"The type of possessions Madam Maria has been doing is not like the possessions you read about or see in the movies. She purposely preys on the weakest individuals, people who are at their wits end, the very depressed, and emotionally lost. A natural demonic possession happens gradually, and the host is usually tormented from the inside, and doesn't move around a lot. The Demon doesn't have too much physical control of the host. As with the possessions that Madam Maria does, she's manually summoning demons and demonic entities and placing them inside of the host, and the possession happens instantly. This is new but even more dangerous because the demons have full control over the host's body, and its bodily functions. So they're running, biting and even in some cases have killed people like a rabid animal."

"So why hasn't Milly been doing that?" I asked but then it dawned on me. "Well technically she has, but why does it come out in spurts? Like she's in control 'now', she seems to be pretty tamed compared to what you're saying."

Jessica took a second look at Milly, examining her head to toe.

"Yes, I can see that, and I don't know why." Jessica scrunched her face and squinted her eyes in deep thought of what to do next. "Milly, stand up real quick," she commanded.

Milly looked over at me, questioning me with her eyes if she should. I nodded my head, nudging her to go. Milly reluctantly rose from the bed, and faced Jessica. Although I trusted Jessica, I too was on edge of what was about to happen between the two. Jessica reached into her back pocket causing both Milly and I to jolt with fear, reaching our hands out.

"Woah! Woah, hey!" I shouted.

"Relax!" Jessica said firmly. "It's just a flashlight," she said, presenting it outward.

Jessica turned on the flashlight and pointed it to Milly's face, who leaned back slightly in discomfort due to its brightness. Jessica leaned in close, examining her face, and eyes.

"That is weird," Jessica whispered.

"What's weird?" Milly asked.

"I don't see the slightest sign of demonic possession. Most of the people who are possessed would have protruding or pulsating veins, bald spots, and bloodshot eyes." Jessica grabbed Milly's hand and propped it up to her face, studying it. "no boney fingers, or sharp nails." Jessica slid her hand from underneath Milly's, letting it fall to her side.

"So I'm not possessed?" Milly asked.

"Oh no, you're definitely possessed by something," Jessica said, flicking off the flashlight. "But tell me, during this 'ritual', do you remember what Madam Maria was saying?"

"Whatever she was saying wasn't English," she chuckled.

"You sure?" Jessica asked. "Not a word? A phrase? A name?"

Milly looked visibly overwhelmed and nervous. She wasn't able to make eye contact with Jessica whose gaze didn't flinch. She looked down at me, as if she was asking for help, but all I could do was shrug my shoulders. I wasn't in the room with her at the time of the ritual, so if anyone would know it would be Milly.

Milly closed her eyes tightly, and forced the words to come out of her mouth. "I think she said "I call upon—" something!.."

Jessica took a step forward with an eager smile on her face. "What Milly? Who?"

Milly sucked her teeth. "It sounded like a pretty name, Diana? Mariana? And that was the last thing I remember before blanking out."

Jessica lowered her gaze to the floor, whispering the names 'Diana' and 'Mariana' to herself repeatedly, as if she was searching deep inside her mind about anything that could come close to those names. She then turned her attention to me.

"And D'Angelo, you said you heard singing when Milly was in your dream right?"

"Yeah" I responded, clearing my throat. "It was faint, but I could hear it."

Jessica patted her thigh, and took a deep breath in, sighing in exhaustion. "I mean, I remember there was an old folklore or legend about a demon named Meridiana"

Jessica paused looking at me, as if she was unsure if she should continue.

"Well, go on," I said. "What else do you know?"

"It's a legend, but I remember hearing that there was a succubus demon, named Meridiana. She fell in love with a guy, who she made pope."

"Since when did demons have a say on who becomes pope?" I asked.

"This was during the medieval period I think, I believe, I don't know!"

"And what the hell is a succubus?" I added.

"Basically, it's a female sex demon, who lures men in, seduces them and kills them when they're at their most vulnerable state."

We all stood still, trading eye contact with one another without saying a word. I figured I had to say what was on my mind.

"Yeah Milly you fit the description."

"Oh shut up!" Milly said.

"I'm just saying you might've been a demon this whole time," I said jokingly.

"Anyways!" Jessica growled, "Meridiana had a beautiful singing voice, and she fell in love with a man who she helped to become pope. One day the Devil came to Meridiana and told her that he did not approve of their love, so he made them a deal. The deal was that the pope couldn't give mass at a church in Jerusalem and if he didn't, the Devil wouldn't kill him and he would let her and Meridiana continue their love."

"Aww," Milly said.

"Aww?" I asked. "This is not cute."

"But I guess he didn't do it right?" Milly asked.

"No," Jessica said, "The Devil tricked Meridiana. When Meridiana went on to warn Pope Sylvester, he and his other demons held her back, not allowing her to tell the Pope."

"So he died?" I asked reluctantly.

Jessica nodded. "But here's where the legend gets crazy, some say that Meridiana was so in love with Pope Sylvester and so distraught over his death that she entombed herself with his dead body. But that's all I can really remember."

"That's so sweet," Milly said.

"It is! Right?" Jessica added.

"Okay!" I interjected. "I like my fair share of toxic relationships but I draw the line there. Jessica, do you think it's Meridiana who is possessing Milly? And is there anything you know that can kill her or a succu—" I paused, not knowing how to pronounce the kind of demon Meridiana was.

"A succubus," Jessica corrected me. "And no, it was just a legend I read about in highschool, I can do some more research at the college library when we get to school." Jessica checked her watch.

"Maybe somebody in your group knows," Milly said.

"That reminds me, Alan, the leader of our group, 'The Eclipse', has assigned me to track you down and kill you myself." Jessica reached into her front pocket.

"Woah" Milly said, taking a step back.

"But I'm not!" Jessica said, while taking out her cell phone. "At least not yet. So here's what's going to happen Milly, I need you to stay with Carla till me and D'Angelo get back from school. Just because I'm the one in charge of killing you doesn't mean other members in The Eclipse aren't after you as well, they already know what you look like, and we know you come here. D'Angelo, they know you're affiliated with her, so I've been told to also keep eyes on you too. They think you're oblivious to the fact that she's possessed, as any sane person would not invite a demon to their house."

"I agree," I added.

Jessica tucked her phone away in her pocket and grabbed her jacket off of my computer chair. "Come on, I ordered an Uber for us."

I snatched my bookbag off of the computer chair seat and placed it on my shoulders. I followed Jessica hastily out the door of my bedroom, but before I could exit Milly called for me.

"D'Angelo!"

'What?"

"What am I supposed to do?"

"You heard her, stay at Carla's for now"

"The whole day?"

"Not the whole day. Just maybe most of it, you know?"

"Oh my god" Milly said while rolling her eyes.

"Shh" I hissed. "Listen, at least Jess is on our side, and we could find a way to help you without killing you."

"Bye Alice!" Jessica hollered joyfully down the foyer. I looked back down the foyer and saw her holding the door open.

My grandma answered her from her room. "Bye dear! Y'all have a good day at school!"

I looked back at Milly standing in the center of my room looking annoyed and extremely tired. I couldn't help but have some kind of pity for her, as she is entirely dependent on me to help, and all she can do is play the waiting game. I rushed over to her and gave her a big hug.

"We're almost there Milly, don't worry," I whispered.

"Okay" she said softly, looking up at me.

"Play nice with Carla."

I rushed out my bedroom door and made my way over to Jessica who stood at the entrance holding the door open with her foot, hurrying me to go.

My attitude had lifted knowing I had an alliance now with Jessica. I had a partner now who was more versed at this situation than I was. I descended down the staircase eagerly, with a sense of excitement and thrill knowing that I have Jessica by my side and some sort of direction to go off of. Fuck Biology class, All I could think about was meeting Jessica later at the library, and learning everything I could about Meridiana and how to put a stop to Madam Maria.

Chapter

FIFTEEN

THE HERMIT

If I'm being honest, I didn't pay attention at all in Biology class, as the only thing on my mind was Jessica. I only played the part of a student, writing down what was on the PowerPoint presentation with a huge grin on my face. To Mr. Carney, I was probably enjoying the lecture, but little did he know, I didn't care, and instead I sat in anticipation for the class to end.

I would've skipped class, a lot of my classes really. But I was already showing up late, and missing every other assignment as it was. Not to mention, my grandma pays my tuition so I'd feel extra guilty for not showing up and getting her money's worth. I've been staying up late nights, struggling to go to sleep, not knowing what might come for me in the night.

When it was time to leave, I packed my bookbag and exited the classroom in one swift motion. I walked amongst the horde of students, bustling in the hallway, but my tunnel vision aimed towards the exit.

I walked outside and onto the beautiful spacious campus. Large and colorful trees aligned the walking paths. I have always loved the campus, as in every season it looked and felt as if you were somewhere upstate away from the city, that was until you'd see the 4 train going by on the other side of the baseball field. As I made my way to the college library, I admired the architecture of some of the older buildings on campus which were made of stone, some dating back to the 1950's but preserved nicely. Despite the cold brisk air and gray skies, the day felt bright and lively.

I went to the second floor of the library and saw Jessica walking towards an empty wooden table, carrying a stack of books in her hands. She placed the books down but before she took a seat, she looked over her shoulder and noticed me approaching.

"Hey there!" she said, with a welcoming smile.

"Hey," I responded, while giving her a hug. The quick casual hug felt right, as if we both needed one at that moment. "Found anything that could help us?"

"Yeah, I did actually!" she said enthusiastically. She pulled out the chair that was tucked under the table and spread out three books that were stacked. She placed her left hand on the book on the far left and spoke to me face to face. "I came across these bad boys here." She lightly slapped her hand down on each book from left to right, "*The Dark Legends of the Dark Ages*, *Mid Century Popes* and last but not least, *Wicca: Step by Step*."

"And you think these books will help?" I asked while circling to the other side of the table.

"It's the best we got, besides, remember what Professor Boston; 'old media is the best media.'"

"Ahh okay!" I responded, I was impressed how she was able to quote our professor at such a time, yet it reminded me of something I forgot to show her, and now was as good of a time as any. I placed my bookbag onto the table and unzipped it, Jessica looked intrigued. "What's the best resource of information?" I asked her.

"A primary resource," she answered.

I reached in my bookbag and yanked out the brown journal I snatched from Madam Maria's house and held it proudly.

"What's that?" Jessica asked.

"Remember when we told you we went back to Madam Maria's house the day after Milly got possessed? I took this, I think it's Madam Maria's journal."

Jessica gasped loudly covering her mouth with both her hands. Her brown eyes dilated above her fingertips. Her reaction alerted some of the other students, causing them to turn around and look at us with concern. At the moment I wasn't sure if I was wielding a bomb this entire time. Thankfully she revealed a dazzling smile from under her hands, and reached out for excitement.

"You took her grimoire?" she asked.

"Yeah, I did!" I said confidently. "Her what?"

"Grimoire, a witch's book of spells and rituals!" she said hastily while carefully taking it from my grasp.

"Oh, then yeah I guess I did." I looked beyond Jessica nervously, concerned that we were causing too much of a distraction.

"D'Angelo, this is badass!" She said while briskly flipping through the pages. "If you take away a witch's grimoire it's way harder for them to conduct magic, at least the more complex ones, and maybe we could know what spells she's been performing." She closed the book and quickly wrapped her arms tight around me.

I returned her embrace and lightly buried my face into her dark curly locks. It was then that I inhaled the soothing aroma of jasmine and amber. The warmth from her hug, and the scent of her hair made me feel as if the daring escapade of stealing the book was worth it. She released her grip on me and took a step back yet her eyes remained glaring up at me in admiration. She retreated her gaze and turned her attention to the table spread of the books. Although she looked away from me, I noticed the curvature of her cheek peeking out behind her hair and knew she was smiling. I was too, probably not as cute and more on the goofy side.

"I'll take a look at the grimoire and *Wicca: Step by Step*, while you take a look at, *The Dark Legends of the Dark Ages*," she suggested.

"Ah, good luck with that" I said, "I took a look in there, it's mostly scribble scrabble in another language, and a whole lot of symbols and stuff."

"That's no problem, I'll see what I can do." Jessica made her way back around to the other side of the table. "See if you can find anything on Pope Sylvester II or anything about Meridiana or succubi in general."

"You got it, chief" I said, while taking a seat in my chair.

Before Jessica could take her seat on the opposite side of the table, her cell phone began to ring. She reached in her front pocket, took it out, and stared at the front screen. The muscles in her face became limp. She looked back up at me and flashed the screen of her phone, while giving me a fake disconcerting grin.

"Gotta take this, I'll be right back" she said.

I watched her walk away and place the phone to the side of her face. She began speaking in a hush tone. All I was able to see on her screen before she walked away was a giant 'A' and a crescent moon emoji. It must've been her boss or leader Alan.

As Jessica crept away into the book aisles, I figured now would be a good time to check in on Milly. I whipped out my phone and called her, hoping for the best. After a couple of rings I heard Milly's sweet sounding voice.

"Hey" she said flirtatiously.

"Hey Milly I just wanted to check up on you to see how you were doing" I said quietly.

"I'm good," she said playfully. "I haven't killed anyone if that's what you're wondering" Milly broke out in laughter.

"I'm glad to hear that, what are you guys doing?"

"Well, we just got done making out."

"Huh?" I paused in disbelief. A moment of silence passed by. "Wh—what did you say?"

"I'm kidding!" she burst out laughing. "Carla went off to the store to get us brunch."

"Okay" I said, rolling my eyes. I was just happy they were doing okay.

"But I have to admit, D," she added, "she's been giving me googly eyes ever since I came back."

The thought of Milly possibly being possessed by an ancient sex demon rang alarm bells in my head. Carla has always taken a liking to Milly, but back at her apartment, Carla seemed to be way more infatuated with Milly than usual. The not so subtle staring, and lack of personal space wasn't something I was used to seeing Carla do. She was more of a subtle hint dropper, kind of like a shy guy who tries to play it cool when they're in front of their crush. I know because that's usually what I do—or try to anyway. If I remembered correctly, Jessica said that a succubus usually preys off of men's lusts and vulnerability. I wondered if the same applies to women.

"Hey Milly, I was thinking, maybe it's best for you to probably lay off the flirting with Carla, just in case."

"Yeah, but I'm not even trying."

"Yeah, I know, I know—" I said rapidly. "But if you have a seductive sex demon inside of you, I don't think we should—you know—rile *it*... or her up?"

Milly didn't say anything, which could be a good or bad thing. She was either internalizing what I was saying or actively trying to come up with an excuse in order to do what she wanted to do. Possessed by a demon or not, I still know Milly like the back of my hand.

"I understand, you're right," she said softly.

Milly couldn't see it, but I looked up at the ceiling and mouthed the words, "Thank God." No back talk, excuses, or jokes. The thought of Carla being hurt didn't sit well with me, and possibly, Milly had the same thought that I had.

A bald man in a blue button-down shirt emerged from the bookshelf aisles and spoke one word to grab my attention. "Hey" he said firmly. He then placed his index finger to his chin and then pointed to the 'No Cell Phone Use' sign, on the wall behind him.

I scrambled in my seat instantly, feeling caught and embarrassed. I apologized to the man and told Milly I'd call her back later, quickly hanging up and slipping it back into my pocket.

As he nodded his head and returned back into one of the book aisles, Jessica stepped out of the other book aisle that was before him, and marched her way over back to our table. She walked with her shoulders back, and pouty lips, as if she meant business and was ready to get to work. Once she made it back to her seat across from me, she instantly dropped her cell phone in her petite leather bag and took a seat.

"Alan wanted to check in, and said that they stopped some guys who were looking for Madam Maria," Jessica said.

"Oh really?"

"Yeah, hopefully with this grimoire, we'd be able to piece together what she's actually up to."

I slid *The Dark Legends of the Dark Ages* in front of me and began my study. The weight and size of the hardcover book was daunting, but I was desperate and there was no time to start getting lazy. I came across one chapter that covered some of the more notable encounters of demons through the Middle ages, which includes kings, peasants, lovers and most importantly, Pope Sylvester II.

Much of what Jessica said about Pope Sylvester II and Meridiana was mentioned in the book, but one interesting detail about the legend was that it is believed that Pope Sylvester II had secretly worked with a blacksmith to create a blessed dagger, should Meridiana ever attack him. With the mysterious gruesome deaths that were plaguing Rome at the time of his papacy, it is also believed he had more blessed daggers made for his clergy and should this 'Mysterious Entity' attack them. Only Pope Sylvester II knew Meridiana was a succubus and took that secret to his death bed, where he asked for God's forgiveness and mercy for his relations with the succubus, Meridiana.

I dove deeper into the mysterious murders during the time of his papacy, and found that there were an estimated 10 to 15 slayings in Rome. Much of the murders were believed to have been of a serial killer or a group of satanists, who mostly killed men in their homes. At first, some of the slayings were so gruesome, townspeople thought it was a beast of some sort that stalked the night. The murders seemed to have slowed down and came to a halt around the time Pope Sylvester II passed away.

Overall Pope Sylvester II sounded like a pretty interesting guy, besides the whole aiding and abetting a murderous demon, not to mention marrying her. It's been noted that he did study and had a fascination with the magical arts before his papacy, which was heavily frowned upon. It seems as though he was preparing to kill Meridiana with these blessed daggers, but there was no note of him ever being physically harmed. The legend says the Devil killed him, while it's believed he actually died of tuberculosis in a matter of a couple of days.

Every now and then, my eyes wandered off to Jessica while she was focused reading multiple texts at a time. I knew she felt my eyes gazing upon her from time to time, as she began to tighten her small lips, as if to hold back from smiling. Sometimes I would do the same and pretend to pay her no mind.

I was so immersed with studying and diving deeper into the legend of Meridiana and Pope Sylvester II, I had lost track of time. It was only until I became mentally exhausted that I leaned back in my seat and rested my eyes for a moment. If Jessica hadn't knocked on the table, awakening me from dozing off, I would've been deep asleep. I was awoken to the sight of her wearing her leather jacket, leaning across the table with a clownish smile spread across her face.

"I wanna try something," Jessica insisted.

"Try what?"

"Come" she said, closing the grimoire with urgency. She promptly hoisted herself up out of her seat, and plucked the grimoire along with her bag off the table. Before I could get up and make sense of how much time had passed, she had already started walking towards the exit.

I shook off the fog in my brain and wiped my eyes, clearing my vision. As I stood up, my legs felt numb due to the extended period of sitting in place, but I persisted, dragging my own book bag off the table, and followed Jessica as fast as my body would allow.

Chapter
SIXTEEN

FOUR OF SWORDS

As we exited the library and stepped out onto the campus, the bright sunlight halted me until my vision adjusted. Through my blurry squinted vision I could still see Jessica marching her way, over to the pedestrian bridge that serves as a walkway over the small campus quad. After a moment, I power walked, catching up just behind Jessica, who still had the grimoire clenched in her hand.

"What is it you wanna do?" I asked.

"Well—" Jessica said without slowing her pace, "I wanna try something Madam Maria wrote in her grimoire, I'll explain just follow me."

Just the idea of mimicking any of Madam Maria's practices made me reluctant to continue on, but Jessica seemed to have known what she was doing. I trusted Jessica, as she wouldn't do anything that would be considered too rash or dangerous, hopefully.

After some time walking along the pathway, Jessica made a sharp right into a small clearing under some trees that was labeled 'The Peace Garden'. 'The Peace Garden' was just a small area surrounded by small white pebbles. Three benches surrounded the area facing its center where a petite two tiered fountain stood at the center.

Jessica slowly approached and stood before the fountain, looking down at its gentle cascading water. As she stood there pondering at the fountain, a small black squirrel scurried across the field of pebbles and climbed up a nearly naked tree, with only a handful of colorful leaves remaining.

"Okay!" she announced, as she adjusted the strap of her book bag on her shoulder. "Grab a handful of stones." Without waiting for my compliance, Jessica kneeled down on one knee and began picking up the small pebbles one by one.

I found the task to be a bit random and wanted to know what exactly we were going to do with said pebbles. With the way my life has been going, I was skeptical of almost anything that seemed normal or safe.

"But—why?" I asked. "Are these magical stones? Is that supposed to be the fountain of youth?" I said pointing at the fountain. "Is somebody buried here? Please tell me!"

Jessica paused and looked over her shoulder at me with her eyebrows raised. She dropped her head forward as if she were fatigued before standing back up and facing me. She leisurely walked over to me, with a grin as if she found a bit of amusement in my paranoid thoughts. My thoughts were far from irrational. They were very much indeed rational as it seems if anything is possible in this realm of demons, witches, and God knows what else.

"D'Angelo—" Jessica said, while taking my hand gently. She turned it over, exposing my palm upwards, "—they're just rocks." Jessica poured a small handful of damp white pebbles and stones into my hand.

I tossed around the rocks in the palm of my hand with my index finger finding no irregularities to your average stone. Embarrassed, I refrained from making eye contact as I walked past her over to the fountain, although I did catch a glimpse of her grin in my peripheral vision. Without further embarrassing myself, I knelt down and began picking up some rocks myself, Jessica followed and joined me. After we both had a handfuls of rocks she stood back up.

"Awesome" Jessica said walking back to the pathway, "we need to make a circle with the rocks!." Jessica led the way and placed the collected rocks down onto the floor one by one, but only had enough to make half of a decent sized circle.

I knelt down beside her and began placing my collected stones alongside hers. "Are you going to tell me what this is for?" I asked. As I laid the stones down, Jessica dropped her shoulder and tugged the opening of her book bag to the front of her, reaching in and pulling out the grimoire.

"Yeah" she said, flipping through the pages. As I laid the last few stones, completing the circle, I rose from the ground and stood beside her. Jessica had stopped on one page, with what looked like a hand drawn diagram of little circles, completing a bigger circle, alongside some small paragraphs that I couldn't make out from afar. "So remember how I said there's a legend that says she entombed herself along with Pope Sylvester II?"

"Yeah?" I said hesitantly.

"Well here in the grimoire, she wrote about how she wanted to see if the legend was real. She connected with some more advanced witches, and one told her a jingle that helps her hear Meridiana." Jessica turned a few more pages with a sense of frustration. "But it doesn't say if it worked or not."

"So you wanna try it?" I asked.

"Yessir!" she responded with eagerness.

"So what's the jingle?"

Jessica flipped back a few pages and cleared her throat. She stopped at one page, squinting her eyes, before reading aloud;

"To sing along with a ballad of bones
Gather nothing more, but only stones
Make a circle to rest your head
As it's the only way to hear the dead.
Knock three times, and knock polite
Only If you wish to hear The Queen of Night."

I took a deep breath, not only to inhale the cool autumn air but also to take a moment to accept the fact that I'ma be placing my face on a ground where hundreds of college students step on every day. On top of that I'm supposedly going to hear an ancient disembodied voice, as if that's not going to give me more nightmares.

"Queen of Night huh?" I asked. "Well if it didn't work for Madam Maria, who's to say it's going to work for us?"

Jessica rolled her eyes, and turned to me. "Who's to say it won't? Besides, if you could go inside a witch's house and steal her grimoire, I think you can do this."

My lips scrunched to the side and my eyebrows twitched upwards, she had a good point. "Fuck it," I murmured to myself. As I descended down to my hands and knees, my head pivoted like a pigeon, wary of anybody looking at me.

"Let me know if anyone is looking," I said.

"You're good, nobody is looking," she giggled. "Don't forget to knock on the ground when you're down there."

I placed my hands on the gray pathway made of hexagonal tiles. I reluctantly inched my face closer to the center of the circle, bracing myself to hear something possibly unimaginably sinister and wicked. I pushed my legs back, flattened my body, resting my chest against the cool ground, and finally my cheek. I raised a fist in front of my face and gave three stiff knocks.

The ambient sounds of the campus increasingly faded away the more I focused on listening to the ground. It was not long before I laid there, waiting anxiously in silence for anything peculiar. Eventually all I could hear was the sound of my heart beat subtly increasing in both volume and pace. But I continued to lie still, waiting for a murmur, a whisper or even a hymn but nothing.

"I got nothing" I said, lifting my head slightly off the ground. The sound of birds chirping and rustling leaves returned instantly as if I lifted my head from under water. I adjusted my body and sat up on my knees, placing my hands on my hips, looking up at Jessica to receive orders on what to do next.

Jessica stood there with her arms crossed, glaring off into the distance, biting the side of her lower lip. Her head pivoted from left to right, surveilling the area once more, before looking back at me. "Let me see," she said sternly, while dropping to her knees beside me. She placed the grimoire on the ground in between us.

I scooted a few inches over to give her some space as she laid down horizontally with zero hesitation. She stiffly knocked three times and closed her eyes. For a moment she waited patiently, just about as long as I had before looking up at me from the ground. From her blank expression, I could tell her effort was futile.

Despite the whole attempt seeming ridiculous from the beginning, Jessica seemed to have been looking really forward to getting some results.

"Yeah, I got nothing too," she said as she pressed her palms against the ground. In a fluid motion, she pushed her torso off of the floor before resting on her knees just how I was. She wiped her palms thoroughly against her slim fit jean covered thighs, before giving me a smirk filled with embarrassment. "I'm sorry," she said shamefully while looking at the ground.

"No, you're fine," I said, rolling my eyes. "It seemed like a cool idea. Imagine if we did hear something!" It was a chilling thought, an outcome that I was kind of hoping that wouldn't come to fruition.

"Yeah, when it comes to these kinds of things, it's honestly worth a shot, because—hey, you never know."

She turned her head to mine and pushed her glossy raven hair back behind her ears revealing her sharp jawline and smooth, warm ivory skin. She looked up at me with her honey-brown eyes, filled with desperation to be understood. She looked at me and paused, followed by time itself. Behind this innocent exterior, coated with an angelic glow, I forgot about the deadly assassin that lays underneath. As I reveled in the moment, gazing into her pupils, a smudge of dirt poked out from the curvature of her smooth cheek, the same cheek she had pressed against the ground. I had lost control of my bodily functions, and instead acted on instinct. I reached out and wiped her cheek with my thumb, gently brushing off the bit of soil. Her eyes shifted to my hand upon my touch and then back into my soul. Her chin began to steadily drop and her lips parted, gently spreading across her face, causing her rosy cheeks to puff up with endearment.

"Yeah, totally" I said, while maintaining eye contact. It felt as if I challenged her to a staring contest, but there was no need—I felt like a winner already.

Before I could say anything else, a rugged sound came from somewhere, disturbing us both out of the moment. Another firm cough caught my attention, snapping my neck to the left, revealing the campus security officer standing a few feet behind us with a disapproving look on his face.

Chapter
SEVENTEEN

THE TOWER

I couldn't speak as the thoughts in my brain seemed to have crashed on their way out of my mouth. I wanted to say something but then again where do I start? It wasn't until having a one-man audience made me understand how intimate the moment was, although all we did was stare into each other's eyes adoringly, while kneeling on the ground; in front of a circle made of rocks.

I looked over at Jessica, who blurted out a laugh before covering her mouth with her hand.

"Whatever you kids are doing just put the pebbles back, please," the officer said. The officer proceeded to shake his head before walking past us, not even bothering to look back. I'm sure he saw his fair share of weird stuff from the students on campus.

"Come on, let's go," Jessica said.

We got off of the damp floor and dusted off our jeans. Jessica put the grimoire back into her bag, as I began to sweep and kick the white stones off of the trail and back near the fountain.

"So other than that did you learn anything helpful?" I asked while kicking the last few rocks.

"Yeah, it looks like our suspicions were true," she said with a sigh. "Madam Maria has several pages of names, most likely they were clientele, god knows how many of them she also has possessed."

"How many are we talking about?" I asked.

"Enough to make a small army."

"Jeez" I said.

"I know, but that's the thing. If she's been collecting this many people, where the hell are they at now? We've caught a few stragglers, but not all these people."

"So you think all these people that are supposedly possessed by Madam Maria are like Milly?"

Jessica squinted her eyes, looked off into the distance in deep thought. "I don't think so," she said finally. "Like I said earlier, the ones we've come across are out of control and violent, as if she couldn't get a hold of them herself. Plus the pages of all the names start way before it seems she took an interest in Meridiana."

"So Meridiana isn't just some ordinary demon, so it might be harder to get control of her," I said.

"Exactly!" Jessica snapped. "I don't think Madam Maria has experience or the power to control, let alone summon someone as powerful as Meridiana. I mean come on, she was dubbed the Queen of Night for a reason apparently."

A sense of accomplishment rushed over me, now that the vagueness of what we've been dealing with is becoming clearer. The phrase, *"if you can identify the problem, you have solved half of it,"* echoed in my head.

"Come on," Jessica said, bobbing her head in the direction of the benches surrounding the fountain. We walked over to the center bench as the stones crunched from underneath our footsteps. As we sat, Jessica whipped her curly hair from out of her face. "So, what did you find?" she asked.

I sat back and took a deep breath, preparing to unload the heap of information I've uncovered in our brief study in the library. "Well, I had to combine bits of information I gathered, from different sources, the book, the internet, and so on." Jessica nodded, intrigued. "Basically I learned a few things, each one kinda filled in the gray parts of the other, but it looks like Meridiana had a pretty high kill count, but those deaths were written off as enemies of the church, or a serial killer", I explained. "Now here's an interesting part of the legend I found on the internet: the Pope supposedly made some kind of blessed dagger, specifically made for killing Meridiana if she ever attacked him. But she never did apparently, there were no bodily wounds at the time of his death. The lore says the Devil killed him, textbooks say it was tuberculosis.

Jessica scrunched her lips to the side, hunching forward, pressing her palms against her thighs. She focused heavily on the fountain in front of us, I could almost see the gears in her head turning.

"What is it?" I asked. For a moment I wasn't sure if the information I shared was at all helpful. "Was that not good enough?"

"No" she said reassuringly as she rested her hand on my knee. "It's perfect, it's just that I remember we might have something like that."

"Like what?"

"The blessed dagger," she answered.

"Really? How?" I asked.

"The Eclipse has a storage room, filled with a lot of old antiques, weapons, and stuff and a lot of it is from missions we've completed, museums, and personal collections. If not that, maybe something similar."

"Okay, but let's say we do have the dagger, or some weapon that could kill the demon inside of Milly, how do we kill the demon and not Milly?"

Jessica didn't say anything, but the awkward silence did. The sounds of birds chirping and honking car horns in the distance filled the space between us. The feeling of hopelessness began to creep into my bloodstream. The enthusiasm of making a breakthrough was swept from underneath me, feeling as if we were back at square one.

"Well here's the thing—" Jessica said, breaking the silence. "If this blessed dagger is true, it might cause more damage to Meridiana than it does Milly."

Just as hope was leaking out of me rapidly like a steady faucet, she shut off the valve. The idea seemed risky, but it's not as intense as shooting her in the head and calling it a day.

"Yeah, that makes sense I guess" I murmured.

"Yeah, I could probably sneak in or ask for some favors to see if they have anything of the sort." Jessica turned to look at me, grinning. "I could go tonight!" She said in a high-pitched voice, followed by a cute chuckle.

"Thank you," I said. "And you can take the grimoire thing back to your 'Base', I'm sure they'll be happy to know you got it."

"Yes!" she said, filled with excitement, clutching her bag. "I can't say I got it from you tho." Jessica pouted playfully.

"That's okay!" I said waving my hand at her. "You tell your boss or leader or whatever that you went into Madam Maria's and found the journal yourself." What bragging rights would I have carrying around Madam Maria's grimoire? They would probably know more of what to do with it than me.

"You're the best!" Jessica said, just as her phone began to ring in her pocket. She took it out and looked at her phone screen with joy. "Hello?" she answered. Jessica twitched her body to the side, and leaned forward. "Uh-huh?" she said.

I thought to turn my head to give her some privacy, and looked at some of the other students on campus walking about their day. It wasn't but a mere few seconds before Jessica reached over and grabbed my shoulder tightly while still on the phone. I looked back at her and saw her jaw wide open, as if she'd been surprised with important news.

"What is it?" I whispered.

In a panic, Jessica began slapping my shoulder while still tightly grasping the phone beside her face. "Okay stand down, don't do anything till I get there!" she barked. Jessica leaped off of the bench, and began to walk to the left of me, causing me to jolt up out of my seat and follow. "Don't tell Alan!" Jessica snatched the phone away from her face, and began typing something on her phone while walking expeditiously.

"Wait what happened?" I hollered.

Jessica whipped her head and body around and gave me a piercing look. "One of The Eclipse members was staking out your apartment, and said they saw Milly on the roof of your building!"

"What?" I began patting my pockets in desperation to find my cell phone. My first instinct was to call Milly, but the adrenaline made it hard to think straight. Eventually I pulled out my phone to check for any text messages or missed calls, but I saw nothing of the sort.

Jessica turned her back and began power walking to the campus exit. "I'm calling us an Uber!"

We raced to the main gate of the college campus, speeding past students and teachers. Upon arrival to the sidewalk Jessica pointed to a single white sedan parked out front, "This one!"

I swung open the car door and stuck my head inside first and asked frantically, "Uber for D'Angelo?" The driver gave me a confused look through his rear view mirror. Jessica touched my arm causing me to look back at her, reminding me who actually called the Uber. "Jessica, I mean" correcting myself to the Uber driver.

"Yup! Get in!" he said.

I took a step to the side and motioned my hand for Jessica to get in first. Once getting in behind her I closed the car door behind me, and snatched my phone out of my pocket as the driver took off. "I'm texting Milly to get inside," I announced.

"No, call her," Jessica ordered.

I didn't bother to argue and switched gears as told and began to call Milly. I pressed the phone to the side of my face. I quickly became more impatient as the phone continued to ring without an answer. I looked over to Jessica who was texting vigorously on her phone. The car stopped at a red light, sending a wave of frustration over me. Jessica must have felt the same sensation as she collapsed both her arms onto her lap and looked up to the windshield.

Jessica adjusted herself before leaning over to the side of the Uber driver. "Excuse me, when you're able to, try your best to drive fast, we're kind of in a hurry."

"Mhm" the driver said. Jessica thanked him before leaning back into her seat.

"Milly's not answering, I'm going to text her" I said. "What did they say about Milly?"

"They said they saw her on the roof with another person, most likely Carla, and they wanted to know if they could move in to take her out. Being that I'm in charge of the case, they have to let me know, and I told them to stand-down."

"And they're just gonna listen?" I asked.

"Hopefully, if anything we can get Milly back inside and out of their sight and say we lost her again or something. Jesus. She couldn't sit still till we got back?"

I was frustrated too, but then something dawned on me. Something peculiar. "Wait, you said Milly was on the rooftop? Probably with Carla right?"

Jessica nodded her head.

"That's not right," I said. "Carla has been inviting Milly to go to the rooftop to smoke weed for a while now, but Milly never went because she's scared of heights." Jessica turned her head to me as if she was beginning to understand what I was trying to say. "If she's on the rooftop, trust me, she is not herself."

Jessica turned her head forward and sat there emotionless like a robot, as if she was replaying all the different scenarios and outcomes in her head. Maybe the gravity of the situation was getting to her, maybe she was locking in mentally and preparing for the worse.

Thankfully we got off of the Cross Bronx Expressway, which was near my house. I looked out the window and saw the sun setting just beside my apartment building in the near distance. As the driver turned the corner on to my block I clutched the car door handle waiting to pull the moment he reached my building.

Jessica looked down at her phone, "They said she's getting aggressive."

"Ah shit" I muttered. I tensed my body knowing I was going to have to make a dash for it the moment I exited out the car. My legs began to twitch up and down ready to take off like a racing greyhound at the starting gate.

"Right here is good!" Jessica called out to the driver. The driver made an immediate stop just a few doors down the block from my apartment building, allowing me to push open the car door urgently.

I ran up the block with Jessica following me closely and darted to the building's front door, whipping out my keys. After unlocking the front door, Jessica and I roughly collided as we forced our way inside the building. I took the lead, running towards the staircase, knowing I was faster than the elevator. I could make it up to 6 flights in under a minute. I'd be out of breath, but I could do it.

I ran up flight by flight, skipping steps and using the staircase's banister to swing me around each corner like a pendulum. I started to lose my breath by the time I reached the fourth floor and my legs grew sore by the time I reached the fifth, but that didn't stop me. Jessica followed close behind, I wasn't sure if she had drawn her weapon out or anything. The only thing on my mind was to stop Milly from hurting Carla. I reached the 6th floor knowing the next flight would be to the roof, preparing for anything behind the door. I've never been to the roof before, so this was a first for me.

"D'Angelo, be careful! Jessica called out from behind me. I noted her request, but I didn't slow down or deter from getting to the roof.

"I got it, I got it!" I panted.

I finally reached a red door leading to the rooftop, knowing Milly and Carla were on the other side. I didn't question anything, I just rammed my shoulder into it, blasting the door wide open. I was met with a gorgeous serene view of a bright orange sky, filled with textured purple and pink clouds. It was heavenly but I had no time to be in awe of the view, as Milly stood to the right with her back turned to me as she faced a terrified Carla near the edge of the roof.

Carla stood there, covering her mouth with the sleeve of her gray oversized sweater, tears pouring down her face sending black streaks of her mascara down her cheeks and into the palms of her hands. She gently swayed side to side as if her body was looking for a way to run, but she was too horrified to move.

Milly stood there with her back turned to me, much like she did the night before when I found her in her room, standing over two dead bodies. Milly was panting heavily as if she was ready to explode at any minute with a blood thirsty rage.

Jessica ran up from behind and joined me by my side with her gun in hand immediately aiming it at Milly. "What is she doing?" she whispered.

"I don't know but it's looking bad" I answered, out of breath. "Milly!" I called, "I need you to gain control of yourself. Whatever you are feeling, I need you to fight it!"

Milly turned her face just slightly looking over her shoulder at us. I could see small red veins protruding from her forehead, just over her red eyes. Her glare didn't last long as she turned her attention back to Carla.

Jessica took one hand off of her pistol and placed it on the large ventilation unit to the right of her. "I'm going to get an angle on her," she whispered. I thought it was a good idea because Carla was too direct in the line of fire If Jessica tried to shoot. Jessica hoisted herself over the ventilation unit and slowly made her way to the other side.

"Milly?" I called out again trying to get her attention, but to no avail. I was losing precious time to get Milly back in control of herself and I didn't have any holy water on me either so I was really defenseless. I know it's not going to take much more before Jessica starts firing at Milly, and The Eclipse is not far behind us either. We were running out of time, and options so why not try something new. "Meridiana!" I said.

I could feel the shift of energy in the air once I said that name out loud. Jessica looked at me with wide eyes as if she wasn't expecting me to say that name either, and neither did Milly apparently. Milly turned her body slightly and finally her head, revealing her face, mangled with illuminating red and black veins. Her face, once filled with intensity and rage, faded away into a face full of sorrow and dread as if she were about to fight back tears. Her glowing pulsating veins seemed to have dimmed down a bit. I had her right where I needed her to be, but I couldn't stop there.

"Meridiana" I struggled to say a second time, "Please don't hurt her, don't hurt Carla." Milly looked back to Carla and back to me on a dime, with a look of disappointment and sadness. I could tell she didn't want to be there, as much I didn't want to be there. I wasn't sure what else I should say. I made contact with a murderous demon. This isn't something you plan for.

I could hear Carla's muffled whimpers through her sweater sleeve. I felt extremely bad for her, as I could only imagine what she had to experience before we got here. This whole thing was partly my fault for putting her in harm's way.

"Meridiana" I continued, "we can talk about this, come over to me."

Jessica's hair flicked in the air as she turned to look at me. "D'Angelo, what are you doing?" she asked.

"Jessica, trust me, I got it!" I said confidently. Honestly, I didn't have anything, I was just stalling and hoping for the best.

Milly took a step towards me as if she lifted her foot out of a puddle of mud. After a second step, the veins on her forehead and face illuminated again causing her to clutch her head in dreaded agony, as she let out a painful screech.

"Help me please!" Milly said, weeping.

I paused for a moment in deep confusion. Those words did not sound like Milly at all. Her voice sounded like a different woman with an echoing and eloquent tone of voice. Did I do or say something I wasn't supposed to?

Carla became startled at the sight of Milly screeching in agony. She began to take small baby steps to the side as if preparing to make a run for it, but it wasn't subtle enough as Milly snapped her attention back to her with a vicious growl, halting her in her tracks. Milly faced back to Carla with her legs bent, and hunched over like a football player preparing to tackle.

That's when I understood that I had officially run out of time and lost control of this rabid creature from hell. A sickening chill was sent up my arms and down my back. I immediately became winded, and couldn't breathe out of fear. A premonition of what was about to happen played in my head vividly. I was too far away as Milly was too far gone, but I couldn't help but try and reach my hand out, as my body pushed towards Milly in a desperate attempt to stop her.

Milly dashed towards Carla with reckless abandon like her life depended on it. Her arms extended forward, and her sharp black talons shredded the air as they moved toward their target. She pressed against the wind, pushing her hair back furiously.

Pop! A sound that drained my face of its blood and knotted my stomach instantly. The sound I feared hearing this whole time, a sound not too unfamiliar in the South Bronx, rang out sending a sonic boom throughout the neighborhood. It was the sound of death.

A single gunshot would stop any man in their tracks, but not Milly, as she just barely curled over in pain. I saw the side of her abdomen recoil where the bullet hit her yet it didn't stop her. She continued on with long strides filled with bloodthirsty fury, before tackling Carla, sending them both over the edge of the apartment building's roof.

The silence of them being out of sight became increasingly deafening, but not as loud and impactful as the thud I heard seconds later. The sight of Milly and Carla falling over the edge of the roof was enough for me to fall to my knees. All hope was lost, WE lost, they were dead, and it was all my fault. I fought back tears and tried to breathe, but instead, I began to sweat and my throat began to hurt as if I had a high fever. Through my watery eyes, I looked over to Jessica who slowly lowered her gun. She looked back to me before making her way over to the edge to inspect the damage.

I pushed off the ground and staggered over to Jessica who clutched my arm. I peeked over the edge and saw Carla and Milly laid out on the ground in the alleyway behind the building, side by side, facing up. Milly's eyes were closed, but Carla's remained open as if she were petrified just moments before death. A narrow dark stream of blood started to flow out of the back of Carla's head, and onto the pavement.

The sight of them both lying dead became unbearable. It was as if my world had crashed down in front of me. My burning sensation scorched the inside of my chest, and my heart pounded against my rib cage. I have never experienced a traumatic pain like this before, the kind of pain that whispered in my ear to join in the same fate as Milly and Carla. Over the edge. My knees had grown weak, nearly making me fall to the ground, or worse, over the edge. With the last bit of light I had inside of me, I shook off daze and stepped away. I was ready to turn and walk away, but just as I had begun to do so, Jessica remained firm in place and tugged my arm back.

"What?" I said, sniffling.

I turned my attention to Milly's pale face and lifeless body or so I thought it was. I leaned in closer to the edge to examine further, and saw Milly's eyes popped wide open followed by her taking a wheezing deep breath in. She swiftly sat up and swung her left arm over herself, gripping Carla's sweatshirt. Milly used the rest of her might to drag herself over to Carla's body and began gnawing on Carla's throat like a watermelon.

Carla's washed out face remained visible just above the back of Milly's head. She couldn't do anything, and with every ounce of my being, I prayed that she didn't feel anything either and her torment was over.

With tearful eyes, I stood there, sick to my stomach and nauseated from what I was seeing. A deep and passionate amount of anger awakened inside of me, not for Milly but for the demon that resided in her.

After a moment, Milly paused from feasting on Carla's throat and with a mouth covered in her blood she looked up at me, flaring her fangs and growling. She crawled away from Carla's corpse like a rabid coyote before running over to a fence. She climbed over effortlessly, and ran off in the neighboring alleyway before disappearing.

"We gotta stop her," Jessica said.

"Yeah, we gotta go," I said, wiping my nose.

The sound of the large metal door startled us both, causing us to jerk around and see what it was. Two men walked through the rooftop door one after the other in all black padded tactical gear with a crossbow in hand. The two men planted their feet in place and stood side by side, pointing their crossbows toward us. Without thinking twice I took a step back and put my hand in the air. I noticed Jessica remained in place almost unfazed at the sight of them.

"Shit," Jessica said.

A large figure stepped out from the rooftop entrance. It was a tall African American man, with long grey dreadlocks with a matching thick gray beard. He was dressed a lot like Jessica, leather jacket, black shirt, but was wearing a large gold cross necklace. His presence alone was authoritative and powerful. I would not want to be on this man's bad side, but considering the grimacing look he gave me and Jessica, we most definitely were.

I understood Jessica not only knew the men in uniform, but she was one of them. He was Alan. And they were—The Eclipse.

Chapter

EIGHTEEN

THE ECLIPSE

One of The Eclipse members had tied a black hand-kerchief around my eyes before we got into a black van, parked outside my apartment building. With a tight grip on my bicep, I didn't bother saying too much, in fear of further agitating them. Instead of putting up a fight and panicking, I listened carefully to their instructions while getting in: watch my head, sit, and don't try anything stupid. After I sat down I could feel someone already sitting to my left as my knee grazed theirs. The member who blinded me with the handkerchief sat to the right of me. Finally, the car tilted to its side noticeably due to the weight of a large person stepping in, followed by the door slamming, which must have been Alan.

As the car took off, the lack of being able to see mixed with the awkward silence in the car, made the ride even more daunting as time went on. It wasn't long before I wondered if they could possibly kill me at any moment, and if so how would they do it. If I wasn't thinking about what horror that lay in my fate, I resorted to replaying the horrors I had witnessed just moments ago before getting into the van. Vividly seeing Milly as a monstrous rabid creature, brutally killing our friend Carla, plunging to her death and devouring her throat. I wasn't sure how I would be able to live with myself after that, let alone be the same person.

I didn't know who these people were and what they were going to do to me or Jessica. I wasn't even sure if she was in the car with me at all. The anxiety turned into self loathing, and I began to wonder if I had deserved whatever awaits me. Despite being in the car, surely filled with god knows who or what, I felt as if I was alone in the world and hated.

I folded my hands together and rested them on my lap and took a deep breath in trying to compose myself. My leg started jumping up and down, and I turned my head side to side despite not being able to see anything. My fear was coming to surface, and I wondered if those who were in the van with me could smell it. But someone did actually, as the person who sat to my left cupped my knee with their hand. It was gentle and smooth.

Jessica?

"Just try to relax," she said calmly, whispering in my ear.

"Hey!" Alan roared, causing me to flinch my hands up out of my lap. "No talking." I could feel his anger and disgust radiating throughout the car. His words seem to have angered Jessica as she tightened her grip around my knee.

With just the crumb of relief that Jessica was able to provide for me, an interesting thought crept inside my head. If Joshua and Carla had fallen victim to being seduced and torn to shreds, why am I still breathing? Why wasn't I put under some hypnotic spell? I've spent the most time with Milly since she had become possessed and she could have killed me easily.

After a sharp turn, the van came to a screeching halt, followed by the van shifting from side to side as Alan exited, slamming the door. I couldn't make out his muffled tones from outside the van, but clearly he was giving stern orders to someone. The sound of the car door to my right opened with the individual clenching my bicep again, dragging me out.

I didn't know where we were, but the air was cool and still. I didn't hear any car horns, rumbling trains, or blaring police sirens in the distance, maybe a little if I focused hard enough. I could only hear the sound of footsteps, car doors closing shut and various insects chirping in proximity to me.

I was then led to the sound of a large metal door opening before me. I entered inside what seemed to be a long hallway, as the sound of mine and many others footsteps echoed along the way. The large metal door slammed shut behind me, followed by the sound of a lock clicking in the distance, sending a chill down my spine. If walls could talk, they were surely telling me that I was officially stuck with no way of getting out now.

I was guided with a hand on my shoulder to make a right and then a short left, before pushing me down, signaling me to take a seat in a clunky metal chair. A moment passes as some more footsteps scuffled into the room.

"What is he doing here?" Jessica asked.

"I said sit in here!" Alan ordered.

"Mista, who is you talking to?" a third familiar voice asked.

"Wait a minute" I muttered.

The sound of another metal chair dragged against the floor screeched as Jessica took a seat to my right. "Okay, everybody stop talking!" Alan demanded. He paused as another door closed nearby.

My handkerchief was pulled off over the top of my head, and I was met with round bulging eyes, staring into my soul from across a table. My vision was blurry as my eyes dilated, but the intensity in his eyes was as clear as day.

He leaned back, giving me a chance to fully observe my surroundings. A pendant lamp hung from the ceiling with a dim yellow glow floated over the table, just above our heads. Behind him was a rectangular glass observation window, and to the left was a thick metal door.

"Ricky?" I said surprisingly. The handkerchief was snatched off of his head.

"D'Angelo?" Ricky sat at the head of the table, with his hands tied behind him. I suspected that he hadn't slept in days with the dark circles around his eyes. He sat in place, anxiously leaning forward like he was prepared to burst out of his seat.

"Oh so you really do know each other?" Alan asked condescendingly.

"Yeah, that's my boy D'Angelo!" Ricky said with pride.

"What is he doing here, Alan?!" Jessica asked firmly.

Alan gave Jessica a disgusted look, gazing at her up and down. His lips quivered and exhaled in annoyance. Clearly he was conflicted about what to say next and maintaining his temper. "I will be asking the questions here, miss gone rogue" he said finally in a grumbling tone. "I want to know what the hell were you thinking taking this entire operation into your hands?" He placed his large hands on the table and leaned forward in front of Jessica's face. "You're not only risking your life, but anyone around you. Look what happened to Tara and Leon, they died at the hands of this— abomination!"

"That abomination is my friend!" I said, puffing out my chest. Jessica turned to me with concern in her eyes. I knew what I said might get me into more trouble, but I had hopes in the pit of my stomach that he would understand if I explained correctly. "Sir, I'm just trying to help my friend, she's been possessed."

"D! No, don't," Jessica pleaded.

"Jessica, he might be able to help us if we just tell him," I said. Jessica put her head down in defeat. Alan shifted to look me directly in my eyes. It was as if I were face to face with a lion, but my bravery roared out as I continued to make my plea. "It's my friend Milly, the witch, Madam Maria, possessed her with a demon called Meridiana! We don't need to kill her we can just—"

"Just what?" Alan interrupted. "Save your friend and kill the demon? Huh?"

"Well, yeah?"

"Not gonna happen" he said, shaking his head vigorously. "What do you think? A simple exorcism gonna do the trick? Huh?"

My words began to stumble out of my mouth. The more I spoke, I started to sound out of my league and possibly even crazy. "No, no—not an exorcism. Do you have a blessed dagger?"

"A what?" He said with great confusion.

I looked at Jessica, and was met with puppy-dog eyes of despair. "A blessed dagger! I researched, maybe you have a weapon that can kill the demon but not the host? A weapon was made for her, Meridiana and if we could just get it—"

"Son, have you lost your mind?" said Alan, making me choke on my own words. "I know what you're talking about, it's just a myth, better yet a legend. A legend that's been passed down through generations, there is no Meridiana! Your friend Milly is possessed, one way or the other, and she is too far gone to even be considered for an exorcism. She has killed two of my men, a girl today, who we are currently cleaning up, and this man's cousin!"

Ricky lifted his head with wide eyes panning from Alan to me. His jaw slowly dropped and his eyes began to water in devastation of being told the truth. The familiar sensation of guilt poured into my gut. I couldn't look him in the eye, so I looked at the ground instead.

"Wha—what? Wait, wait" Ricky mumbled. The revelation of information was a gut punch to him. "What is he saying D'Angelo?"

Jessica shot to her feet in protest. "Alan, why the fuck would you say that?"

"Why the fuck would I? Why the fuck would you? Any of you? All of you are in over your heads!" Alan paused. "Kid, look at me." With all my might, I garnered the strength to look back up at him. And beneath his hard and rugged exterior, he seemed to have switched gears to be more empathetic, calming his voice down and relaxing his face. "You care about this girl. She's your friend, I get that, but you can't let your friends drag you down. You're not a hero, kid. How many people is it gonna take to get hurt, or die before you learn to let go?"

His harsh words burned deep inside of me, and the look on Ricky's face was only the icing on the cake. I couldn't breathe, I barely wanted to breathe at that. I was hit with a harsh reality check of all my mistakes and choices. I trembled under the weight of my guilt, and had no choice but to sit there like an idiot in front of Jessica, and a lying traitor to Ricky.

"Did you bring Ricky here just to tell him that?" Jessica asked.

"No, your man Ricky here almost ended up like Milly actually. We found him by the Grand Concourse asking around for Madam Maria, before we brought him here. He got a little rough, that's why we had to restrain him."

I looked over at Ricky from across the table and was met with a glaring stare filled with hate and disgust. I couldn't blame him, I would feel the same way.

The sound of a walkie-talkie sounded in the room, causing Alan to reach for his hooked to his side waist band. "Go for AL," he said. The walkie-talkie was too low for me to clearly hear, but Alan paused in deep concentration with the walkie-talkie placed to his ear. "Got it, we're on our way, stand by." Alan pressed a button on walkie-talkie, making a beeping sound, and placing it back to his mouth. "All available personnel, report to the lot! I repeat, all available personnel, report to the lot!"

Jessica stood up once again, "What? What is it?"

"Surveillance team said they found Madam Maria, and a bunch of her possessed victims in Pelham Bay Park, there's a whole swarm of them."

"Okay, let's go!"

Alan stuffed his walkie-talkie back onto his waistband. "No, *we're* gonna go," he said, pointing to himself. "You— all of you—are going to stay here till we get back."

"Well, why can't I come? I'm a part of this team."

"Are you?" Alan said, pointing his finger at Jessica. "I don't trust you right now! Members of this team don't go off the radar and do whatever the hell they wanna do." Alan's eyes scanned the three of us fiercely from right to left and back again. "Like I said, you all stay here." Alan turned away and opened the door. Before walking out, he turned around and gave me one last look. "I'm sorry kid but if I see your friend, I'm taking her out like the rest of them. Nothing personal." Alan stepped out, closing and locking the door behind him.

I looked on and watched multiple armed men jogging past the observation window. Their marching footsteps faded away along with their echoes. The silence was uncomfortable, but not as uncomfortable as Ricky's hollow stare into my cranium, yet I had no choice but to let it fester inside my brain. I was too ashamed and scared to look at him.

"I'm sorry guys" I professed, slouching into my chair.

"Sorry for what? Lying to my face?" Ricky began to raise his tone. "For protecting that bitch?"

"Ricky, chill," Jessica said. "He didn't know she was possessed when she killed your cousin!"

"Yeah but he obviously knew after the fact!" Ricky fidgeted and rocked around in his chair, but thankfully his restraints kept him in place.

"I didn't ask for any of this!" I answered. At that moment, I was tired of feeling scared and guilty. The past week has been hell, and I've been scrambling non-stop trying to find a solution, and neither Jessica or Ricky understood the risks that I have taken to fix things. I was at my boiling point. "I was only trying to do what was right! I was trying to save Milly's life, and all that did was cause more trouble."

Ricky stood up with his hands still tied to the back of the chair. Jessica stood up putting out one hand in fear he'd charge over. I nearly forgot how big and tall he was as he'd become even more intimidating while being angry. "But why didn't you just tell me bro? Do you know how much pain that has caused my family?" Ricky's voice cracked with pain and anger.

"What was I supposed to say?" I cried out standing up. "Hey Ricky, Milly might have eaten your cousin alive because she's possessed by a demon. You'd look at me like I'm crazy or beat my ass thinking I was making a joke."

Jessica clasped her hands together and took a deep breath. "Okay guys, look—we all wanted to find a solution to this. Ricky, D'Angelo was trying his best to help Milly, and here's the thing, it wasn't really Milly who did this, she was possessed! and if you were in D'Angelo's shoes, you'd do the same thing, protecting your loved ones. And, since you were looking for Madam Maria, who knows you could've ended up just like her or worse." She then turned to look over at me.

"D'Angelo, Ricky is just getting hit with *all* this information right now, so of course it just looks like it's your fault but it's not." Jessica walked around me and stood in front of the window with her head held low. "It's Madam Maria's fault." Jessica leaned her back against the window and rolled her eyes. "And now The Eclipse is gonna fight her and her possessed minions, possibly killing Milly, and I'll probably get fired or God knows what they would do with me."

I slumped back down in my chair. "I'm sorry, Jess—"

"—Don't apologize," she said. "It was my decision, I didn't have to go along with it. Besides, part of me always wanted to find cures and help people instead of just hashing and slashing. There's some innocent people shrouded in darkness who just need a hand up, you know? Or maybe a second chance." Jessica didn't make eye contact with anyone, instead her eyes fluttered around from the floor to the ceiling, which told me she was speaking from the heart and felt some type of shame.

Ricky sat back down in his seat and sucked his teeth. He sat there blankly staring at the table with his chin tucked to his chest. "I get it, all of this is that witch's fault" Ricky said nodding with foreboding anger. "D'Angelo, all I'm saying is—" Ricky looked up from the table and over to me. "—I would've believed you bro." Beneath Ricky's anger, the tone of his voice revealed he was just truly disappointed in me. "Yeah I would've been mad, or upset but at the end of the day, I would've been like, 'let's go get that bitch together.'" This whole time I thought she'd be able to help but really she was the one who caused all of this."

I didn't see the flames in his eyes anymore, I saw my friend Ricky talking to me like a brother. I stood up from my seat, and carefully walked over to him. He stood up and the legs of the chair tied to his wrists flared out from behind him. He gave me an icy look as he towered over me, but I knew it was safe as I saw the corner of his mouth grin. I gave him a much needed hug. "I'm sorry, bro," I said.

"I'm sorry too," Ricky said. "I would hug you back, but—the chair," Ricky said laughing.

"I got it," Jessica said delightedly. She walked confidently over to Ricky, and reached in her back pocket, retrieving a tactical knife that flicked out the blade by the push of a button. She was able to cut the rope in one fluid motion, instantly dropping the chair, freeing him.

"You could've done that 10 minutes ago," Ricky said.

"I could've, but you probably would've choked out D'Angelo and I didn't wanna risk it." Jessica said jokingly.

"Smart," Ricky said, nodding. Ricky turned and gave me a big strong bear hug lifting me off of the ground, making me groan a little in pain. I knew it was purposeful as he probably had to let out some of his left over animosity still in his system. He dropped me back to the ground after I tapped him on his back to let me go. "Get in on this Jessica" Ricky said, draping his arm over her shoulders and pulling her for a group hug between the three of us. A hug I think we all needed.

As we untangled our arms from around each other, I was relieved, yet the joy I felt didn't last long when I realized we were still stuck in this room until god knew when.

"So—are we just gonna wait till your group gets back?" I asked Jessica.

"I mean, I guess" Jessica answered, walking over to the door. "This door can only be open from the outside." She leaned her back against the observation window and crossed her arms and legs.

"What if they don't come back?" asked Ricky.

Judging by Jessica's face, it was a question I don't think either of us wanted to ask ourselves, entertaining the idea Madam Maria could very well annihilate Alan and the Eclipse. We don't know what Madam Maria has in store for them. Who knows what she's been able to conjure up since we've last seen her. Ricky looked down at us like he instantly regretted asking the question himself.

Just behind Jessica on the other side of the window, I noticed a white figure begin to walk out of the darkness and into the light. The more I looked the more I was able to clearly see a white short-sleeve shirt and khaki pants. But what elated me was seeing a familiar kind face and a neat gray beard.

"Oh shit, no way," I said, stepping forward.

Jessica jerked her head up to me. "What?"

"Wait, who is that?" asked Ricky, joining my side.

Jessica swiftly turned around and looked along beside us.

"Theodore!?" I said with a big smile.

"D'Angelo! How are you son?"

"Wait, you know Theo?" asked Jessica.

"Yeah, he's a family friend," I answered. "What are you doing here?" I asked.

He stood there with his hands in his pockets, calm, cool and confident as if he was proud to see me. "Oh I'm just passing through. Thought I might lend a hand where I'm needed."

"How long have you been standing there?" Ricky asked.

"Oh, long enough."

"Wait, why is he here?" I asked Jessica in a hush tone.

"He used to be a member of the Eclipse, but he's retired, he still passes from time to time to say hi," she answered.

"Really? Him?"

"The glass is bulletproof—not soundproof," Theodore called out. "Here." he walked over to the door, unlocking

it from the outside and pushing it open. "I've seen all I've
needed to see—I think you guys are ready."

Chapter
NINETEEN

SEVEN OF WANDS

The three of us rushed out into the long, dark, ominous hallway like cattle, scrambling to roam free. My mind raced with questions; *which way was the exit? What to do first? Why the hell was Theodore here?*

"I'm really glad to see you Theodore," I said.

"Likewise, D'Angelo."

Ricky spoke up from behind me, "Hey, mister, what did you mean when you said we were ready?" A statement that I caught onto as well when he said it.

In his smooth, jazzy voice, Theodore answered, "oh, well I couldn't let you guys out with negative spirits. What good would that have done?"

"So you saw the whole, hugging thing?" asked Ricky.

"Mhm"

"And the whole, 'protecting that bitch' thing?"

"Ricky!" Jessica said, "we're running out of time. We have to go to the storage room."

"What do you need in there?" asked Theo. "Never mind, I'll come with you." Theodore put his hand on Ricky's shoulder. "Ricky, is that your white Honda Civic outside?"

"I think so," Ricky answered.

"I know so, we only drive black cars" Theodore said, holding up his car keys to his face. "Meet us out there, while we go to the storage room" Theodore said, pointing to one end of the dark hallway.

"Oh!" Ricky squealed, snatching the keys out from Theodore's hands. Ricky didn't hesitate to jog in the direction Theodore pointed. His words echoed in the distance, "They better not have scratched my car! *Ay dios mio*."

Theodore then placed his heavy hand on my shoulder and guided me to turn around and walk with him in the opposite direction. "Okay, what do we need in the storage room?" he asked. I could still hear his calm tone of voice, but I sensed the urgency deep within.

Jessica marched alongside us. "Do we have any daggers, or weapons dating back to the middle ages, or even renaissance?"

Theodore didn't say anything as we marched along the dimly lit hallway. Jessica ran ahead to a green door on the right and burst through it. Theodore didn't release his grip on my shoulder the entire way over. I wasn't sure if he was guiding me, or just using me as support, maybe both.

The storage room was fairly large, with a few shelving units, packed with a variety of boxes, crates and containers. Some boxes were stacked on the floor, some were stacked high enough that it would require a ladder to get to. As I walked in, Jessica snatched a box off of the second shelf of the first shelving unit, and viciously moved around the contents inside. Theodore let go of my shoulder and he leaned against the door frame.

"Any idea of where to start?" I asked.

Theodore stood there in deep thought, scratching his beard. I couldn't wait, I had to scramble and move fast like Jessica and look for something, anything. I walked in between two shelving units and began to read the label's on the boxes and crates, hoping something would point me in the right direction. '*Louis–1800,*' '*Iron Urns,*' '*Roman Medal.*' Half of the labels looked like chicken scratch to begin with. I was unsure to open each box and stick my hand onto some cured object. Jessica didn't seem to mind though, as she was on her second box, pulling out wrapping paper.

"Wha—wait wait!" Theodore called out. "The bottom shelves against the walls- they have a lot of old heavy weapons from the middle ages if I remember correctly."

Without questioning I slid to my knees and scurried over to the bottom shelves in the back wall at the end of my aisle. There laid medium to large sized slender wooden crates, each with a small white label the size of a business card. I read the words, "*Swords–1400 AD*", but then "*Swords–1000 AD*" caught my attention. "Hey, I think I got something!" I called out while pulling the crate off the shelf and onto the floor.

"You think you found it?" Jessica asked.

"We'll know when we open it. Get a crowbar."

After catching my breath from pulling out the heavy crate, Jessica came back with a red crowbar and stood beside me. "Watch out," Jessica warned as she jammed the edge of the crowbar inside of the crate, and began to press down. I noticed she had difficulty pushing down, breaking it open, so I placed my hands beside hers and pressed down along with her, snapping the crate open.

I pushed off the lid and was amazed at the sight of two real medieval swords sitting in a bed of straw. They both looked grainy, rusted and oxidized. I would be cautious to wield them as I would fear breaking them, but they were indeed two heavy pieces of metal nonetheless. Beside them laid what seemed to be a smaller sword, with a broken handle piece. If only these objects could talk, I could imagine what these blades had cut through back in their heyday.

"Nothing!" Jessica hissed.

I sat back for a moment and pondered which one should be the next crate to open. There was one more crate, deeper and to the right of the storage shelf that caught my eye. "Hold on," I said as I crawled over. I poked my head inside the storage shelf, squinting my eyes to see the words on the next crate, which was made of a darker and more weathered looking wood. On the card it said '*Medieval Church*' which was enough for me to give it a try. "We gotta try this one!" I dug my knees into the floor and pulled out the heavy crate from the shelf with all my might.

"What's this?" Jessica asked.

"It says, 'Medieval Church.'" I finished pulling the wooden crate out making a loud thud as it hit the floor. As the adrenaline pulsed through my veins, preparing to open another crate, I looked over to the door, and noticed Theodore was nowhere in sight, but we had no time to wonder why.

Jessica slammed the crowbar under the lid of the crate once more. "You ready?"

"Yeah, on the count of three" I answered, placing my grip on the crowbar, beside hers. "One, two, three!" We pushed the crowbar down together hard in unison, making the lid nearly fly off entirely.

I looked down into the crate and saw various sacred items, resting on cushiony red velvet material padding. I again found myself reluctant to touch anything, this time out of respect. I didn't need to rummage around the crate, nor did I need to open another one. Alongside a thick wooden cross, a gold brittle chalice, and a bible, sat a dagger still snuggled inside its sheath.

The dagger was practically calling out to me, making the hairs on my neck stand up. The silver cross design on the handle of the dagger was the icing on the cake letting me know, if there were ever a dagger belonging to Pope Sylvester II, it was this one. Jessica looked over at me as if we struck gold.

I carefully grabbed the dagger out of the crate and grasped the sheath, sliding it off. The blade looked to be in great condition for it to be about a thousand years old. I'm no weapons expert but the sides of the blade seem to be a bit dulled out, but the tip remains pointy enough to do some damage still. The grip was made of gold, with a silver cross on both sides.

"That's the best we got," Jessica said, hastily standing up.

"Yeah, I'll take it," I added.

I placed the dagger back inside its sheath and followed her to the door, where Theodore emerged from around the corner. He raised both his hands, one holding both of our bookbags and the other, Jessica's gun. "Did you find what you were looking for?" he asked.

"I think so! Thanks Mr. Theodore" Jessica said as she retrieved her belongings.

"Yeah, thank you," I added. The sound of a radio frequency screeching in the distance caught my attention before stepping out. "Wait, what was that?" I took a step backwards in the storage room and looked behind me, to see where the noise was coming from.

"There!" Jessica said, pointing to a lone walkie-talkie on a desk to my left. She marched over to it, snatching it off the desk and began adjusting the volume and frequency. "Maybe we can hear Alan and find out what's happening. Hello? Hello?" she called out. She placed the walkie-talkie to her ear but nothing but radio interference. "Alan! Do you hear me? Anybody?"

"I was telling him to get new walkies," Theodore said under his breath.

Jessica began to hit the walkie-talkie with the palm of her hand. "Eclipse, does anybody have eyes?" she cried out. Me and Theodore paused and looked at each other with matching concern.

A scratchy radio signal screeched out through the walkie-talkie, followed by Alan's voice filled with urgency. "Any available personnel, report—!" The walkie-talkie went quiet.

"Do you read me?" Jessica called out. The walkie-talkie remained silent, frustrating her enough to slap it repeatedly. "Damn it, we gotta go!"

"Right!" I said, "Theodore, you coming with us?"

Theodore smiled and shook his head gently. "Oh no no no" he said. "I'd be more of a liability, if anything. You two go! I believe in you!"

"Okay, okay" I said, taking my backpack. We rushed past him and ran down the dim hallway. I turned around and saw him standing in the pool of light coming from the storage room. "Thank you Theodore!" I called out.

"No problem, and please, call me uncle Theo!"

As we continued our way down the poorly lit hallway, I focused on the large metal door at the end. As we approached it, I braced myself because I knew, once we were on the other side of it, there would be no turning back, and we'd be set on our way to fight Madam Maria—and only God knows what else.

Chapter
TWENTY

THE CHARIOT

I rammed the door open with my shoulder, and was startled by the sight of a large man standing there in all black. I squealed—a manly squeal, of course—and balled my fist in front of my face, ready to fight if needed. Thankfully he took a step back, and I noticed it was actually Ricky. I hunched over and leaned on my thighs, catching my breath.

"Oh shit, it's you," I said.

"Yeah it's me! What did you think it was?" Ricky said in shock.

"I don't know. I wasn't expecting you to be right—there!"

Jessica walked out calmly, giving me a confused look. "You okay?" she asked.

"Yeah, I—I just wasn't expecting Ricky to be right here when I opened the door" I explained to her.

"Well yeah, I was about to come inside to see what was taking you guys so long," Ricky said. "Did you get what you needed?"

"Yeah," I answered. As I caught my breath, I took note of my surroundings, and noticed we stood in an empty parking lot outside. It was dark out, and the crickets and cicadas were singing. I saw a white Honda, parked behind Ricky against the chain link fence next to a light box. "That's your car, right Ricky?" I asked.

"Yeah, Let's go!" Ricky answered. "You guys know where they at?" Ricky took out his car keys from his jacket pocket and pressed the button to unlock his car.

"All we know is, it's at Pelham Bay Park" Jessica answered. "I'll stay on the walkie and see if I can connect with someone. I'ma open the gate for you, Ricky." Jessica made her way over to it.

I got in the passenger seat, followed by Ricky getting in the driver seat. Once he drove the car to the lot's front gate, Jessica pushed a green button on a gray box mounted next to the sliding gate, allowing it to slowly open. "She's one hell of a woman, huh?" Ricky asked.

"Mhm," I replied, while admiring her from inside the car. While she stood there waiting for the gate to finish opening, she looked over her shoulder and looked directly at me as if she felt it. I started to wonder how our eyes are able to connect to one another so effortlessly, like twin flame telepathy.

Once Ricky was able to drive out and onto the street, Jessica closed the gate behind herself and got in the rear passenger seat. We drove down the dark street that was lined with a tall wooden fence and thick weeds on one side. Eventually the wooden fence came to an end and opened up to a beautiful view of the East River and the White Stone Bridge whose bright lights shone in the distance. It was a peaceful and dreamy sight to behold at such a moment. I didn't wanna say anything as I didn't wanna disturb the moment, and I think Ricky had the same idea. *Enjoy it while we can.*

Once the scenic view of the water and bridge was out of sight and behind us, Ricky drove onto the New England Thruway, heading north to Pelham Bay Park. The road was smooth and not too crowded with other motorists, thankfully.

The car ride allowed my mind to wander off, reminiscing the moment of unsealing the crates with Jessica just moments before. It reminded me of a similar time where I attended Milly's cousin's birthday party when I was about thirteen years old. There were two Piñatas, one for the kids, and another for the adults. I remember we were a little too old to fight amongst the younger kids so we had to elbow our way through with the adults. There wasn't as much candy in our Piñata, so we'd be lucky to get a handful each. But I had collected a generous amount of candy off of the floor. I looked over and noticed Milly had probably three pieces at most, she was too busy laughing hysterically at the sight of her older relatives rough housing each other on the floor for some candy. The kind of laughter that would always make my day. I scooted over and presented my pile of candy, offering for her to take it.

"Aww" Milly said, as she pouted her bottom lip.

She reached into my pile taking a few of her favorite pieces, which was anything sour. She loved sour. She could've taken the whole pile, I wouldn't have cared. I was never much of a candy eater anyway.

I shook off my daydream and started to put my game face on, because at any minute, the next exit we would take would bring us to Madam Maria.

I couldn't get over the fact that Theodore was part of The Eclipse. He didn't strike me as a guy who dealt with demons and the paranormal. He was way too tranquil and smooth for that field of work. You would think someone with that background would be a lot more like Alan— rough around the edges, combative, or strict. I figured now was as good of time to ask Jessica, who seems to be on pretty good terms with him, calling him Theo and all.

"Hey, Jess" I called. "What's the deal with Theodore being in The Eclipse?"

"Oh Theo is mostly retired from The Eclipse. He used to be a high-ranking moth back in the day."

"Moth?"

"Yeah, a group of Moths is called an Eclipse."

"Ooh!" I said with pure joy. The explanation behind the name tickled my brain as if I had solved a complex puzzle.

"Yeah," she continued. "He retired a long time ago, but he still comes by from time to time".

"Good thing he came today I guess," I said.

Jessica agreed.

"Do you know what exit I should take?" Ricky asked, breaking his silence.

"I'ma see if I can get someone on the walkie," Jessica answered.

Pelham Bay Park is the largest park in New York City, contrary to what many think that title goes to Central Park. It's not as famous, nor is it around the corner from some of the city's tourist attractions, but it's a staple in Bronx culture. If you haven't had a family barbecue there, or visited Orchard Beach, could you really say you grew up in the Bronx? Pelham Bay Park was big, you had the barbecue area, the beach, the track field, but much of it still was either open land or forests that nobody really goes into.

"Does anybody read me? This is Jessica!" she said. The walkie-talkie went silent as she paused waiting for a response. A low unintelligible voice came through the walkie and went silent. "Hello anybody?" Jessica called out. Static came through the walkie followed by a female voice in distress.

"Jessica—is that you?" said the voice.

"Yes! This is Jessica—is this Debbie?"

"Yeah, it's me, where the hell are you?" she cried out.

"I'm on my way!" Jessica answered loudly, "Where are you—Pelham Bay Park?"

The static continued, and no voice came through the walkie-talkie. I turned around in my seat and saw Jessica who was intensely staring down at the walkie, hoping for a response.

Ricky looked up into the rear view mirror. "We're coming up on the first exit, do I take it?"

Jessica looked up at the front windshield, and fidgeted around in her seat. "Uh—hold on, hold on" she said anxiously. She placed the walkie back up to her mouth and spoke, "Debbie, location?"

Ricky fidgeted around in his seat, constantly looking in the rear view, and side mirrors. I could understand his anxiousness. Every second counted and one wrong exit could make us too late to reach The Eclipse in time. I was also partially concerned that we'll get into a car accident with anybody else on the highway with our antics.

The car started to merge onto the right lane, preparing to take the exit. "Come on, come on, come on," he muttered under his breath. It was now or never to take this exit.

The static sound coming through the walkie paused, causing our stomachs to drop into our laps. "Shore Road!" the walkie cried out.

"Ricky get off the exit!" Jessica screamed.

Ricky aggressively turned the car to the left, sending us all in the car tilting to the right. Ricky's sharp turn caused his tires to screech, driving over the white gore lines dividing the main lane and the exit, nearly missing the yellow reflective crash cushion. Ricky regained control of the car, and continued on his way.

"Oh shit, everybody okay?" he asked.

"I think so!" I answered. "You, Jess?"

"Yeah I'm okay. Two more exits," Jessica ordered.

Ricky nodded and continued on his way down the road. We didn't speak much about the near death experience we just had, but I could tell we were all spooked and on edge from it. I had to roll down my window to get some much needed air, and clutched the grab handle above my shoulder. It wasn't long before we were pretty much the only ones on the highway, and the road became increasingly dark and desolate.

Ricky later took the appropriate exit off the highway, this time much more smoothly like a landing jet plane. Ricky slowed down when we started to drive on a dirt road and eventually came to a complete stop once we came to a fork in the road with a green sign in the middle, detailing that to the right is Cove Pier, and to the left is Shore Road. We were surrounded by dense woodlands packed with tall trees. My head began to turn on a swivel, as I became more intensely freaked out by our surroundings.

Ricky knew which way to turn, but I think anxiety started to set in for him. He took a deep breath and began nervously patting the steering wheel before firmly grasping it before turning to the left and proceeded down the road. "*Ay dios mío*, here goes nothing."

Ricky continued down Shore Road. The silhouette of trees riddled in darkness was as far as the eyes could see. Besides the car's headlights, The bright moonlight was our only ally, aiding us in our adventure into the night. I didn't hear any outstanding noises, only the tiny woodland creatures could be heard.

"You think she gave us the right directions?" I asked openly.

"Let me see," Jessica said, grabbing her walkie. "Debbie, are you there?" more static came through the walkie, followed by the sound of a female's voice grunting and gasping for air as if she was hurt and running. "Debbie, who is with you?" she asked.

"What the hell is happening?" Ricky asked.

"I don't know!" Jessica answered.

A bright flashing light lit up the night sky like lightning, just over the top of the trees ahead of us, silencing us all instantly. The light source was probably a mile or less, but its presence definitely let us know we were on the right track.

Ricky put his foot on the gas driving faster, and with more confidence, knowing we were just around the bend from joining The Eclipse and fighting Madam Maria.

"Okay, do we have a game plan?" I asked.

"Show up and take 'em down," Jessica answered, cocking back her pistol. "Speaking of which, do you still have the dagger?"

"Yeah," I answered. I reached into the smaller pocket of my bookbag that sat between my legs on the floor of the car, retrieving it and holding it up for her to see.

"Good, give it to me," she said, sliding it out of my grasp.

"But wait, shouldn't I be the one to—you know?"

"If Milly is there, she's too dangerous right now for you to get close to her." I've taken down a few demonic beings before and we got one shot with this, and we still don't even know if it works."

Jessica's math did make sense, but she had a gun and several knives on her. An alarming question rang in my ear, what did I have to protect myself?

Before I could speak another word, the road ahead opened up and we saw several black sedans and vans parked ahead. The sound of muffled groans and screams alerted us all that we had arrived. Ricky slowed to a stop, inspecting the area, as Jessica leaned forward in her seat, perching her head in between us.

Jessica pointed to the first van on the left hand side, which sat beside a slope. "There! Pull up to that car" she ordered.

As Ricky slowly approached, the horrific screams increased in volume. I poked my head forward, looking over the dashboard to get a better view and saw a scattered mass of people fighting in what seemed like a war taking place—and the good guys weren't doing so well.

Chapter
TWENTY-ONE

STRENGTH

I bolted out the car door without a second thought and ran in front, followed by Ricky and Jessica. I looked over the cliff and saw the horde of people fighting in a clearing below. Some looked human, some not so human. I was able to make out those who clearly belonged to The Eclipse, from their padded uniforms and others with black leather jackets and like Jessica. From a distance they looked like they were fighting people who were deranged and out of control, and others were humanoid beings but leaner and taller, hairless and with gray skin.

Some lifeless bodies from both sides remained scattered in various spots of the open field. I saw one man crawling away from the battlefield and into the surrounding woods.

The Eclipse were holding their own, but they were definitely outnumbered, and wouldn't last for long.

Ricky joined me to my left side. "Shit." he hissed. "What the hell is this?" He looked on in despair.

Jessica joined my right side. "Fuck, we gotta help them."

"Help them?" Ricky asked in a high pitched voice. "Help them how? What the hell are those—things?" With Ricky frozen in place, and his voice cracking in fear, I grew worried that he had begun to have second thoughts on the matter.

In the midst of the bloody and hellish chaos down below, I was glaring down like a hawk scanning for any sign of Madam Maria or Milly. A bright flash of light caught my attention from the dark woods behind the battlefield, followed by someone running out and away from it.

Jessica pointed to the man who emerged out of the woods, "That's Alan!"

He looked weak as he walked with a limp, clutching his stomach and out of breath.

Once in the clearing he turned back around and faced the dark woods where he just escaped from. A possessed man in tattered clothing ran up to Alan, swiping at him. Alan dodged the blow, grabbed the man's arm and performed an arm drag takedown, followed by stomping down on his face. Alan continued to look forward hunched over with balled fists, waiting for someone or something to step out.

A small figure dressed in loose red garments stepped out from the woods, where Alan had previously ran out from. A bright ball of light sped from the small figure to Alan, blasting him away a few feet, sending him on his back.

"And that's Madam Maria!" I called out.

Alan gingerly rolled over on his side and stood back up, regaining his fighting stance. He looked hesitant to take another blow from her, as he began to take steps backwards. He was clearly hurt, limping like an injured animal, desperately trying to survive.

Madam Maria's stride didn't flinch in movement as she continuously approached Alan like she was toying with him. She paused in her pursuit and began to glow red, as did two other possessed individuals nearby Alan, who soon ran after him with their arms fully extended outwards.

Alan punched the first one in the face and threw him to the ground. He then pulled out a knife from his side and stabbed the second one in the head, knocking it to the ground. Alan fell backwards onto his buttocks and started crawling away.

"We have to go down there and help!" Jessica said.

"I'm staying my ass up here" Ricky said with glassy eyes.

"I'll go down there myself!" Jessica said, whipping out her gun.

"Woah, woah" I said, grabbing Jessica's shoulder. "No you are not!" I wasn't going to let us split up, especially to go out and fight alone. I was tired of being scared. I was tired of this world bullying me. I saw this as the moment to fight back, but if we were going to fight we had to fight together. "Guys, this is the moment we've been waiting for!" I turned and grabbed Ricky by both of his shoulders. "Ricky, this is the moment *you've* been waiting for! Think about the pain Madam Maria caused your family. Think about Josh!" Ricky finally averted his eyes from the battlefield and down to me. "You wanted to avenge your family right? This is it! You don't have to fight alone because I'm here to fight with you!" I stuck my hand out for a handshake. "Me, you and Jessica, bro. We can make this right." Ricky looked down at my empty hand, but didn't say anything. I understood, this was more than what Ricky had asked for, I couldn't blame him for feeling he was too small for this fight.

Ricky turned away, left me hanging, and walked back to the driver side door opening it. I dropped my arm back down in defeat. I looked back at Jessica, who was clearly frustrated with Ricky's dismissal. Ricky tucked his head inside and the trunk of his car flew open.

"D'Angelo, come here," Ricky said, nodding his head. Jessica and I followed Ricky and stood in front of his open trunk. "If we are going to kick some ass we can't go empty handed." Ricky reached inside, and unzipped a large duffle bag, revealing several aluminum baseball bats. "My uncle likes to play baseball on the weekends. I'm sure he'll understand if we borrow these."

Ricky took out one bat and handed it to me and then another to Jessica. He took a third bat out and rested it over his shoulder, before closing the trunk and giving me a smirk and fist bump.

"Okay! Let's go kick some ass!" Jessica roared with enthusiasm as she made a run for it.

"Woah, woah, mami" Ricky called out to her, stopping her in her tracks. "I got a better idea, get in."

Jessica walked back to me as we were both confused about what the plan was, but then it clicked. We all rushed back inside the car. I lifted my book bag to make way for my feet but I wondered why I felt the weight shifted around like liquid. I opened the large pocket and saw a couple of filled up water bottles that I had not placed in there. After I pondered how and why they got there, I had realized those water bottles were actually a gift.

Ricky reached for his phone and started typing. "You know I might die today—" he said, turning up the volume to max on his dashboard, "—but I'll tell you what. I ain't dying without good music. This is for you, Josh!" Ricky began to play a loud latin rap song, before reversing the car and sped down the hill and to the battlefield.

As we closed in on the fight, I noticed Alan was on the ground with one of the larger and more demonic looking humanoid demons standing over him preparing to strike down and kill him. I pointed, directing Ricky to drive to him. I rolled down my window and climbed half way out, sitting on the car door. I looked over the roof of the car and saw Jessica following my lead on the opposite side of the car in the rear passenger window with the bat in her hand. With my left hand clutching the grab handle for dear life, I pulled out my bat and aimed for the demon's head. Once we were close enough I swung my bat as hard as I could. Direct hit! The demon's head went flying off. I was elated at the fact that I actually did such a thing. Jessica looked proud of me from across the roof of the car, cheering me on. But then it dawned on me.

"Oh my God—did I just kill someone?" I asked.

"Don't think, just swing!" Jessica called out as she swung her bat as well, knocking another possessed person's head off.

I was slightly nauseated, but she was right. I couldn't think too much, thinking too much would get me killed. After just nearly passing a few Eclipse members, Ricky hit a possessed woman head on, sending her toppling over the roof of the car between me and Jessica. I know she was possessed and all but damn, I still just saw a woman get hit with a car. Geez, man.

I shook off the daze that clouded my head, and swung again, this time hitting another possessed man in the head, knocking his head off as well. It started to feel like hitting mailboxes with bats. It's getting easier, still not easy, but easier nonetheless.

Jessica seemed to be in her element, fiercely and joyfully knocking the heads off of evil beings, while hanging out the window of a car. "Wooo" she cheered. One after another, she was striking them down on her side.

I looked forward and saw another slim build hairless demon coming up. I cocked my arm back preparing to swing and knock this demon's head into next week. Just as I was prepared to swing, Ricky slammed the car's brakes, forcing my arm to swing and losing my grip of the bat, causing it to fly over the hood of the car.

"Sorry!" Ricky called out. "There's people in the way!"

I looked ahead in front of the car and noticed a few of the Eclipse members on the ground either laid out or crawling to safety. I couldn't be mad at Ricky, I would've done the same thing.

I looked over at Jessica, who seemed to have lost her bat as well. "You okay, Jess?"

"Yeah I'm fine," she said, ducking her head back inside the car.

We both sat back down in our seats to regroup. I saw my bat just ahead of the car, and I pondered if I would actually make it if I ran out of the car to go get it back.

I frantically didn't have much time to think as a large monstrous hand reached inside through my car's window and clutched my shirt with great strength. Jessica and Ricky screamed and I'm sure I did too. The arm and hand that gripped my shirt was large, gray, hairless, and boney. The finger nails were pointy, yellow and long. I grasped the cold wrist of the demon, and tried to slip away from its hold desperately. Ricky took his bat and began striking the forearm with the knob of his bat but it remained unfazed as it began to pull me out the car's window.

I pushed and tugged, trying my best to yank myself away from its grasp, but it didn't budge. Instead it only raised me higher and looked at me face to face. Its eyes were milky white with pin drop pupils, with deep sunken in eye sockets and thick structured cheekbones. Its teeth were sharp and yellow with blackened red gums. Its dense, hot, smokey breath reeked of rotting flesh. It looked into my eyes as if it had despised my very existence.

A loud gunshot blasted, and the head of the demon snapped to its right, releasing its grip, dropping me to the ground. The demon slowly tilted over and fell like a tree being chopped down. I turned over on my back and saw Jessica standing just over me, with her gun still pointed forward.

"You okay?" she asked.

"Yeah, thanks for the save."

Ricky turned down the music in his car and leaped out with his bat in hand. "D'Angelo, you good?"

"He's fine," Jessica answered. "Ricky, behind you!"

Without hesitation, Ricky raised his bat and swung behind him, hitting another possessed person viciously in the head, knocking it to the ground. I could hear its skull cracking on impact with the bat. He swung his bat down two more times, making sure it was dead.

"Thanks. These are some ugly motherfuckers," He said, catching his breath. "D'Angelo, get your bat, I'll cover you!"

"Okay," I agreed. I stuck my head and torso inside the car window, reaching inside my bag to retrieve a large water bottle. With the water bottle in hand, I dashed over in front of the car and made my way over to the bat. I could hear Jessica's gunshots ring out from behind me. Once I picked up the bat I turned around and saw Ricky running towards me, but another possessed man shoulder tackled Ricky from the side with great impact like a football player, sending him to the ground. He began to strike down on Ricky with closed fists, as Ricky was just barely able to defend himself, blocking the strikes with his baseball bat.

I ran over behind the possessed man straddling Ricky and unscrewed the water bottle cap, dumping some water onto his back. The possessed man leaned backwards, screeching in pain. Smoke rose from his back and his flesh began to burn. I saw the perfect opportunity. I dropped the water bottle to the ground, and swung the bat down on the possessed man's head as hard as I could, sending him toppling over on his side.

I offered my hand out to help Ricky up off the ground. "You good brother?"

Ricky snatched my hand and pulled himself up. His body weight almost pulled me down instead. "Yeah—the fuck was that you used?"

I reached down and picked up the water bottle off the floor, tossing it to Ricky. "Holy water," I answered.

Ricky held it in his hand, rotating it around in awe. "Wow, I could use this."

"I know right?" I answered.

I took a second to look at the possessed man now motionless on the moist ground floor. Up close I could see he was as ugly and deranged as Jessica described the other possessed people she has come across. Despite him and a few of the others looking like a walking corpse, some of them possessed athletic agility and strength.

Jessica shot her gun several more times, getting my attention. She stood in front of the car with her bat perched up against the hood. She shot almost anything possessed and demonic in sight. She was a good shot with it honestly. She went to shoot once more at a possessed man approaching her, but nothing fired. She stuck the gun in the back of her waist band and snatched the bat beside her, swinging with full force knocking one of the possessed men down and out.

Before she was able to notice, one of the larger hairless demons rushed up to her, grabbing her by the throat and slamming her down to the ground.

"Jessica!" I called out painfully.

I ran over to her, tightly gripping the handle of the bat, concentrating all of my energy and focusing on my next swing. I wasn't just angry, I was honestly scared. Scared of Jessica getting hurt or possibly worse. I didn't want that to happen, I couldn't let that happen. I gripped the bat so hard it hurt my hands. With all my might, I swung as hard as I could. If it was a baseball, I would've hit a homerun and then some. When the bat hit the demon in the back, I probably broke its ribs, as it groaned in pain.

But I knew I couldn't stop there. I began to see red. I hit the demon a second time, and then a third time, hitting everywhere I could. Each blow made a clunking sound making the demon moan in pain. I lost count of how many times I struck down, before I finally bashed its skull in.

By the end I was gasping for air and took a knee, leaning on the bat for support. After a moment I looked up and saw Jessica leaning against the car, gently caressing her chest. I didn't want to look away from her as her eyes spoke peace back into me. She was okay.

We staggered over to each other, meeting up halfway. She looked up at me as her eyes sparkled in the bright moonlight. It was then that I understood—I didn't wanna play it cool anymore. I didn't wanna play it safe. I didn't wanna be 'Mr. Nice Guy' anymore either.

"D'Angelo, that was awes—"

I leaned in and kissed her lips soft but passionately. Her small, slightly parted lips were soft and warm. The touch of her lips eased my racing heart. I slowly drifted away and our eyes met as they both steadily opened together. Before I could drift away too far, her petite, cold hands cupped my face and pulled me in for a longer kiss. I gently rested my hands around her waist. With the amount of force she pressed against my lips, I could tell she had been craving for this moment for about as long as I have. But overall it was a moment that felt right.

Once our lips parted from each other, we looked into each other's eyes again, like neither of us wanted this moment to end, but of course there's always a cockblocker.

"Aww, how precious," a familiar rickety voice spoke, causing me and Jessica to separate in fear. Madam Maria emerged from the darkness. "Long time no see D'Angelo, how have you been?"

"I think we're way past asking you to stop huh?" I said.

Madam Maria chuckled. "You always were the smart one."

"You!" Ricky called out from behind us. Ricky marched his way over, dragging the bat along the dirt, "You want to fuck with my family?" Ricky raised his bat over his shoulder, preparing to swing at Madam Maria.

"Ricky stop, don't!" I said.

Madam Maria put her hands in front of her, creating a red ball of energy. With a subtle push of her hands, the energy ball shot out striking Ricky, launching him several feet back.

Madam Maria laughed hysterically. "Oh please Ricky, your cousin Joshua, was but a mere piece of the puzzle. His life served a greater purpose—my purpose."

"What the hell is all this for Madam Maria?" I asked.

She laughed again, as if this was all a game to her. "For the power of the night, of course!" she squealed. "Think about it! I have the power to reach down in hell and give demons and revenants a vessel to walk the earth more easily. But under my control!"

Another red ball of energy formed in front of Madam Maria, and hit both me and Jessica, sending us flying backwards. The blast felt like a big push, as the landing was what hurt the most—knocking us on our asses, and knocking the wind out of us both. We groaned in pain and rolled over on our hands and knees.

Madam Maria continued to walk towards us. "I can make an army!" She hissed. "And what better way to do that, than having the original Queen of Night herself at my disposal! Speaking of which, I think I have someone here who wants to see you."

Madam Maria looked to her right and into the dark woods. A red glow flashed in the darkness behind the trees. The wind picked up and an icy breeze sent a chill up my spine. Madam Maria began to laugh louder and harder, relishing in the evil she conjured. A dark silhouette of a person formed behind the trees, stepping out into the moonlight. That silhouette became Milly.

Chapter
TWENTY-TWO

HAIL TO THE QUEEN

Milly staggered out of the woods, hunched over and with her head down. A red glow pulsated from underneath her skin, like evil coursed through her veins. With each step she huffed and groaned in exhaustion with the ground trembling beneath my feet. Her aura exuded power and most of all danger.

"Isn't she wonderful?" Madam Maria asked. "Meridiana used to instill fear into the hearts of kings and rulers, plaguing kingdoms with nightmares and fear. Sadly she never reached her full potential, but together we can make that happen."

Something seemed off about Milly compared to the rest of the demons we've fought. The others didn't possess the same glowing energy as she did, nor did she seem as free as the rest of them, like she was on a leash. I saw the fault in Madam Maria's plan.

"You don't have full control of her—do you?" I asked. "I think you bit off more than you can chew!"

Madam Maria's smile had vanished. By the deathly look in her eyes, I could tell I pointed out her weak spot. Or at least hit her ego.

"Oh D'Angelo, always intuitive. I had trouble summoning Meridiana, yes! She's very powerful, even without a thousand years of feasting on human flesh, but little by little, with each time I force her to kill, not only does she become more powerful and embedded into Milly's body, the more control I have over her. And what's a better way to finish the job, than her killing the white knight himself."

My body became stiff as I became petrified with fear. I was now next on the menu. I felt as if I was being watched—better yet, starved after. I turned around and saw the rest of Madam Maria's possessed army standing in place, scattered around the clearing, all staring at me like an audience. Too many to fully count in the darkness. It wouldn't surprise me if there were more somewhere in the woods.

"Or D'Angelo, one of your little friends would do?" Madam Maria said, glancing over to Jessica and Ricky.

The thought of Madam Maria hurting another one of my friends enraged me. I couldn't let that happen. There was no time for me to be scared. I had to act fast. I looked at Jessica's side and noticed she still had the dagger in its holster to her side. That was our ace in the hole. She nodded to me, as if she was ready to act on the plan we agreed on.

"I'll cover you," I said.

Jessica leaped to her feet with the bat in her hand and swiftly ran over to Milly. Milly's red hue intensified as she raised her head and saw Jessica approaching. With all her might, Jessica swung her bat, aiming for Milly's head, but Milly was able to catch the bat's barrel effortlessly. Jessica stood there astonished at Milly's strength and speed. Jessica began to tug the bat away, desperately trying to pry it from Milly's firm grasp.

Milly drove her foot into Jessica's stomach, pushing her off while snatching the bat out of her grip. She swung the bat, but Jessica was able to narrowly dodge it by ducking under. Jessica landed two firm punches to Milly's chin followed by a roundhouse kick to her side. Milly flared her fangs, roaring like a tigress.

I looked to my left and noticed one of the possessed men started to run over to join Milly in the fight but I wasn't going to allow that. Just as he reached me I extended my leg, tripping him. It was as if he paid no mind to me at all, and continued to crawl and inch his way over to Jessica and Milly. I adjusted the grip on my bat and began to beat down aggressively on his back and then finally his head, caving it in.

A heavy hand landed on my left shoulder, causing me to instantly swing before I could think that it was another possessed person or demon. My wrist was caught briskly on my swing, and noticed the hand belonged to Alan.

"It's just me, son!" he said.

"Oh, sorry" I said.

"Thanks for buying me some time," he said.

"Uh—no problem."

I looked over his shoulder and noticed the remaining members of The Eclipse continued to fight the possessed, including Ricky. It looks like we bought them some time to get back in the fight.

"There's still some possessed hiding in the woods, they've been spilling out since we got here, god knows how many there are, we gotta put an end to this!" Alan said out of breath.

"Jessica has the dagger we've been looking for!" I said. "We have to help her."

Alan paused and gave me a tense look. I don't think he liked the idea of us relying on the use of a magic ancient dagger. Alan exhaled, swallowing his grievance with the idea, and placed his hand on my shoulder, nodding.

Together we turned our attention back to Jessica and Milly, finding Jessica crawling backwards on the ground, trying to get away from Milly, who was still wielding the bat in her hand. Simultaneously we rushed over, side by side. Milly raised the bat over her head preparing to strike down on Jessica like an axeman chopping wood. I lunged myself forward and slid on my knees, holding the bat horizontally above my head blocking the blow. As her bat collided with mine, a loud clang echoed in the distance and the vibrations traveled past my hands and down my arms.

"Milly I know this isn't you!" I said as I struggled with the pressure she forced down onto my bat. "We're gonna get you out of this I promise! Just hold on!"

Milly looked down at me with wide fiery eyes. Behind her demonic rage, I was still able to see her for who she truly was. The crushing weight that I once carried on my shoulders was now just inches away from my face. A sharp pain shot through my wrist. I wasn't sure how much longer I would be able to hold back the pressure Milly forced down upon me. Thankfully I had some help.

Alan kicked the center of Milly's chest with his large boot, sending her backwards a few feet. Milly dropped the bat to her side and pulsated another red glow, growling in anger. With a head of steam she lunged at Alan like lightning, grasping onto his leather jacket like a spider monkey, giving him one stiff head butt, knocking him to the ground. Clutching his leather jacket, she roared in his face, flaring her razor sharp fangs. She released her grip, and slashed his abdomen with her claws tearing through his shirt. She raised her other claw, tensing her fingers, preparing to strike down again.

A splash of water dosed her from above her head making her screech and arch her back in pain. Steam arose off of her body like a pot of boiling water. Ricky stood behind her with an empty water bottle in hand. With a sadistic smile on his face, he tossed the water bottle to the side. Milly locked eyes with me, taking deep, slow breaths filled with rage.

"I'll show you—" Ricky raised his bat over his shoulder, "—what happens when you fuck with me!" He swung his bat as hard as he could. With a balled fist, Milly raised her forearm to her side blocking Ricky's bat. Ricky staggered back from the recoil. "Oh shit" He said.

From the look in her eyes, the holy water only enraged her. She slowly stood up and turned to face him, as he stood there in fear, not knowing where to run. Ricky dropped his bat and turned to run away but Milly appeared out of thin air in front of him, grabbing his throat. Ricky squirmed in agony trying to breathe. She held onto his throat, squeezing tighter and tighter, forcing Ricky to his knees.

I ran over and stood beside Ricky, bat in hand, hoisted over my shoulder prepared to swing. I froze when I saw Milly's face. Beneath the deathly glare she was giving Ricky while choking him, and the dark veins spread across the side of her face, I saw someone who I loved, someone who I protected, someone who I'd never harm. I couldn't bring myself to swing. It was almost like she didn't notice me while she was focused on squeezing the life out of Ricky. I had to stop her another way.

"Milly stop! Please!" I pleaded. "Come on!" I could hear the last bit of air in Ricky lungs leaving his body. I grabbed her forearm and began tugging it as best I could with her strength. "I don't want to hurt you!" In a last effort, I raised my bat again over my shoulder, and adjusted my grip. Before I could swing, she steadily turned her head to look at me. She let go of Ricky's throat, who fell to the ground gasping for air. With her eyebrows raised, her eyes had become glossy.

"You were going to hit me?" she asked, taking steps towards me. "What—what did I do to you? I thought we were friends, D'Angelo." Her voice began to crack, fighting back tears. I took steps back, keeping my distance. "It's me, Milly," she said, reaching out her hand smeared with blood.

I was deeply confused and scared. My hands had become numb holding the bat over my shoulder, but I didn't lose my stance as I inched backwards. I saw Milly, I heard Milly, but it wasn't her, I reminded myself. "It's not you, stop this game Meridiana, Madam Maria, whoever you are!"

Milly paused in her steps and dropped her arm to her side. She wiped her nose and sniffled. "I remember when we were kids, you said you would marry me one day. I remember, one day after school, you gave me a box of chocolate for Valentine's Day and a card." Milly giggled, wiping her eyes, painfully smiling.

Those were memories and feelings that I had locked away over the years. I remember how much I romantically cared for Milly as we grew up as kids just going about life. Her words, her tears, reached into my chest and clawed out my innermost secrets and desires, and I hated it. "Shut up, shut up!" I demanded tearfully.

"I was such an idiot back then, I'm sorry. Maybe we can still do that, D'Angelo. You and me." Milly took another step towards me bridging the gap between us.

I looked down again at her blood soaked hand, and noticed the blood began to soak into her skin. I started to awake from my emotional trance when I saw her eyes start to glow red. A sinister smile carved into her face. Her innocent laugh that I fondly remembered evolved into a wicked one, one much like Madam Maria.

Milly began to speak, but it was Madam Maria's voice. "Let's go D'Angelo, let's go and get married" followed by another sinister laugh. Her laugh stopped, and her eyes and voice returned to normal. "I'm sure your grandmother would love to see me," she said. Without warning she kicked me in the stomach, sending me to my knees. "All will bow before me!"

Without looking away, Milly snapped her hand out to her side like lightning, swiftly catching Jessica's wrist, whose hand was holding the dagger, the blade inches away from her stomach. She glared at Jessica in disgust and snapped her wrist to the side, making her cry out in pain as she dropped the dagger to the ground.

"What is this? A present? For me?" Milly asked. "Oh you shouldn't have. But I have some bad news to share with you, Jessica." Milly grabbed Jessica by the throat. "Me and D'Angelo are going to be moving on, without you." She then hoisted Jessica in the air by the throat.

I saw the dagger just in front of me, I knew what I had to do. The dagger was practically calling out to me. I was nauseous and weak, but I reached out and slapped my hand down on the ground, grabbing the dagger. I looked up and saw Jessica's feet dangling in the air to the right of me and Milly standing with her arm raised sturdily in the sky like a statue. I saw my opening, and I took it.

I yanked my arm back and swung the dagger as hard as I could, piercing Milly in the stomach. Milly gave me a look of a wounded surprise with pitiful eyes, the same look I've been dreading to see this entire time. She released her grip on Jessica's throat, causing her to fall to the ground beside me. I fought through the pain and stood up, looking at her face to face.

I tried to pull the dagger out but it wouldn't budge. I took my other hand and placed it on her shoulder. As I pushed her away and slowly yanked the dagger out, Milly took a step back, and fell to her side, but some kind of ghostly dark matter remained where Milly once stood. The more I looked in front of me the more the figure formed into what looked like a person, forming arms and legs, then a body and head.

As hard as it was to not look away, I saw Milly on the ground motionless to my right. I peeled my eyes away, and went to check on her. I knelt down beside her and gently shook her shoulder. "Milly? Milly?" I called out. I looked down and saw a large spot of blood on her shirt where I stabbed her, continuing to grow in size.

A hard thud hit the ground, grabbing my attention. I saw a woman in a black dress, with long wavy hair draped over her face, on her hands and knees. The skin on her exposed shoulders and hands looked pale with a tint of gray and blue. Chains were wrapped around her wrists and forearms. Black smoke arose from around her, like a live fire. This was for sure the demon that possessed Milly—Meridiana.

Chapter
TWENTY-THREE

DEATH

"What have you done?" Madam Maria cried out.

Honestly, I asked myself the same question. I didn't know what just happened, nor was I expecting this.

Meridiana huffed and groaned while facing the ground in exhaustion, as she slowly lifted her head and the hair that veiled her features parted like curtains. There, I was able to see her black eyes with a red streak beneath them falling down to her sunken cheeks. The tips of her fangs peered out just over her red lips.

Like a wounded animal, she clawed at the ground, making her way towards me. She seemed weak, scared and desperate even. Her blackened eyes somehow radiated pain and misery. As she had gotten closer to me, I had begun to smell the pungent odor of coal and burning wood like a campfire. Just below her chin, I saw a link chain dangling from her throat, swaying side to side with each stride she took.

She looked over to Milly by my side, tilting her head examining her. She slowly reached her shaking left hand to Milly's head.

"Don't hurt her," I demanded, causing her to flinch and retreat her hand back a bit. She looked at me and shook her head. She carefully reached her hand out again and caressed the side of Milly's head.

"Kill them! Kill them now!" Madam Maria cried out. I looked over my shoulder and saw her clutching her loose garments in desperation.

A pillowy hand with a sandpaper texture cushioned the top of my forehead, startling me to look back at Meridiana. Her large glowing yellow eyes were hypnotic. A sudden yellow flash blinded me momentarily, and my body and mind were overcome with a rush of joy and the thrilling sensation of a smooth rollercoaster.

As my eyes cleared, I was greeted to the sight of a tall beautiful woman, with long dark curly hair in a red flowy medieval dress. Her jawline was sharp and her nose was petite. Her eyes were kind and her lips were plump and rosy. Her beauty was nearly intimidating the more my vision cleared.

Behind her was a scenic view of a lake, with a large orange sun setting behind it just on the lake's horizon. I looked around and saw we stood in a tiny clearing surrounded by tall dense trees. Butterflies fluttered through the tall grass and the birds could be heard singing in the trees. All I could smell was the sweet aroma of flowers and morning dew. It was a dreamy serenity.

"What the—where am I?" I asked.

I was no longer on the battlefield fighting Madam Maria's army. At least not consciously. I was somewhere far away, safe, tranquil and dream-like.

"D'Angelo?" A voice called out from behind me up a small hill. I turned and looked in between the tall trees. She stumbled out of the depths of the forest and had an elated look on her face. "D'Angelo!"

"Milly?" I answered. She hurried down the hill with open arms and tightly embraced me. She looked fine, she looked whole, she looked and sounded like herself again. I tightly wrapped my arms around her in disbelief and didn't want to let go. "Are you okay?" I asked, grabbing her shoulders and looking into her eyes.

"Yes!" she answered joyfully.

As we embraced again, I rested my chin on the top of her head and looked over to Meridiana, who stood before us with a soft, joyful smile. I tapped Milly's shoulder to detach from me, pausing our reunion, as we both turned to look at Meridiana in unison. I was happy and joyful, but I wanted to know what all this meant.

"Don't be alarmed," she said. Her voice was smoothly innocent and enchanting. "But we don't have much time."

"So, are you really Meridiana?" I asked

She nodded her head with a grin. "Please understand, I did not wish for any of this."

"I don't think any of us did truthfully," I responded.

She took a step forward and clutched my arm gently, looking deep into my eyes. "D'Angelo, you are truly remarkable, a noble young man indeed."

"Thank you," I said.

She giggled. "You remind me of someone. Someone wise and brave. Someone who I cared for deeply once upon a time." I could hear the pain in her voice. She then gently placed her hand on the back of my neck, and rested her thumb on my ear, tilting my head and leaned forward with a glassy look in her dark eyes. "Please continue being the *light*, and please—" she raised her other hand, cupping her chest, "—aim for the heart", she whispered.

She vigorously tugged my neck back, sending me falling into a dark abyss. My heart sank and couldn't breathe. The longer I fell, the darker things became until it became pitch black and I couldn't hear anything, not even my own thoughts of panic. My stomach dropped once again, giving me a nauseating feeling.

I opened my eyes and was jolted with the feeling of anxiety and energy. My ringing ears adjusted back to normal, with the sound of Madam Maria calling out in the distance. The ghastly version of Meridiana returned in front of me. Her glowing yellow eyes dimmed back to black as she pulled her hand away from Milly, slowly panting in exhaustion. Mentally, I was now back on the battlefield.

"What are you doing?" Madam Maria called out. "Slaughter them, I say! Return to your former glory!" Madam Maria paused and silence blanketed the area. I looked around and saw everyone had stood still, the demons, the possessed and The Eclipse, all looking at us. "You will do as I say!" Madam Maria roared.

The chains and cuffs on Meridiana began to tense up and illuminate a reddish glow. She screeched in pain, opening her arms wide to sides, exposing her nearly decayed rib cage with a glowing pulsating red heart, tucked beneath an opening. She dropped her arms, pounding the ground with great force. She lifted her arm and cocked it back preparing to swipe down with her sharp talon like nails.

I clenched my grip around the dagger, and locked my sight on her red phosphorescent heart. I closed my eyes and with all my might, I swiftly jabbed forward, beating her to the punch. On impact, she let out a sharp painful and pitiful squawk that echoed in the distance. I opened my eyes, witnessing my hand holding the dagger, piercing her chest and heart. I yanked the dagger out, briefly disgusted with the black blood on my hand and the sloshing sound it made as I pulled back.

Meridiana rested her striking arm, lowering it back to the ground. The light illuminating from her heart dimmed out as did the chains that imprisoned her. She choked and coughed up a little black blood from her mouth while giving me a painful smile filled with gratitude.

"What happened?" Madam Maria called out, rushing over to us. "You fools! what have you done to the queen?"

Madam Maria slapped my forehead and began kicking me with her red slippers. "How dare you! I'll kill you myself! I swear."

A deep gurgling growl eroded, pausing Madam Maria in her tantrum. She looked over her shoulder, finding Meridiana tense and on all fours like a tiger ready to chase its prey.

"Yes! Yes! Yes!" Madam Maria said filled with joy. She bowed and opened her hands to me as if she was presenting me as dinner. "Here, your highness! Show him who is the true Queen of Night."

Meridiana didn't move as she sat there looking forward to Madam Maria. In an instant she flexed her arms, breaking off her restraints and having them fall to the ground. Like a snake, she smoothly stood upright on her legs.

"What is it?" Madam Maria asked hesitantly. "You may—feast upon this pathetic fool, all of them, there's—"

The ground beneath us began to shake. Meridiana took a step forward, startling Madam Maria to cautiously take a step back. Madam Maria stood hunched over in fear, not knowing what to do.

"Meridiana please!" Madam Maria pleaded, "We can take over the world, the night can be ours—yours again! You just have to-" she looked at Meridiana's feet and noticed they had begun to slowly sink into the earth like sand. Meridiana lifted her foot from the dirt and took a step forward, and that foot too continued to descend into the earth. Madam Maria looked back up to Meridiana with a sinister wicked grin. "Too bad, looks like you've run out of time," she snickered.

"No—" Meridiana hissed, "You did."

Madam Maria lost the smirk on her face and began to run away as fast as she could. Meridiana lunged to the ground on all fours and began chasing after her. Madam Maria slid past a possessed man, using him as a blockade, but Meridiana plowed through him with ease with just a swing of her arm, snarling in frustration. Meridiana continued her pursuit across the field kicking her way through the sinking dirt surrounding her. As Meridiana closed in on her target, her lower half began to fall into the earth, but that didn't stop her from clawing at the soil, trying to advance forward. Meridiana screeched in desperation as the dirt reached up to her chest just as she was just a few feet away from Madam Maria.

Madam Maria turned around taking strides backwards, and enjoyed the view of Meridiana's last moments of sinking into the earth. She clutched her chest, and took deep slow breaths, snickering in sweet relief.

With just her head and shoulders floating above ground, Meridiana stretched out her arm, hopelessly trying to reach Madam Maria, as if it was her dying wish. As she inched closer, her head submerged into the dirt followed by the rest of her arm and finally her hand. Meridiana was officially out of sight and the rumbling ground subsided.

Madam Maria joyfully clapped her hands and laughed wickedly. "Oh happy day!" She said, hopping with joy. "The old goat couldn't do it then—I guess she couldn't do it now." She sighed, calming down. She started walking towards me with a confident stride. "You see D'Angelo? You see what happens when you try to give someone a helping hand? You try to pull them up and they try to pull you down!" Madam Maria broke out in laughter.

Jessica sat up with her hand cupping her throat, "D'Angelo what's happening? Did you do it? Did it work?"

"I think so—but we are not out of the woods yet!" I answered.

I looked around and saw all of the remaining possessed people and demons scattered all over the field, all looking at us with dead eyes. Some more began to wander onto the open field from the forest.

Madam Maria closed in on me as she approached. "It was all fun D'Angelo, but now you and all your friends, everyone you care about must d—." The ground began to shake again and rumbling could be heard beneath me. We all looked around in confusion.

Meridiana erupted from the earth between us, like a shark breaching water, kicking up a cloud of dust. Madam Maria turned to run away but Meridiana was able to grab her ankle, tripping her to the ground. Madam Maria dug her nails into the soil—grasping and clawing at the dirt and grass.

"No no please! I'm sorry! Don't do this!" she cried out for mercy.

Meridiana didn't let up. She continued to pull Madam Maria relentlessly down into the dirt with her, tugging and tearing into her loose witchy garments. Madam looked at me in misery and reached out her hand for me to take it. I locked eyes with her as she was swept away and shook my head.

"No! Please!" she cried out as the last bit of Madam Maria was gone.

The area was at a standstill. None of the possessed moved a muscle; they all just stared where Madam Maria perished underground. One possessed man in a dingy white button-down shirt fell to his knees and groaned in pain, clutching his head with both hands followed by another possessed woman in the back. Jessica watched along with me as one by one, they collapsed to the ground, moaning and groaning, before finally laying still on the moist ground.

The tall gray demons had combust into flames that slowly ate away at their thin frames. As the flames consumed them, their ashes flew away with the wind and only their bones remained.

Jessica rose to her feet and groggily made her way over to the possessed man who collapsed nearby.

"Jess!" I called out in concern.

She put her hand in the air, halting me. She knelt down and began tugging his shoulder before flipping him over on his back. She leaned her ear down, and listened to his mouth. After a moment, she swung her head back. "I think he's going to be okay!" she said surprisingly. She looked over her shoulder and scanned the field of what used to be plagued by a possessed army.

"You think—all?" I called out. I could see Jessica's pearly smile as she nodded with enthusiasm.

Milly! What about Milly? I wondered.

On my hands and knees I scurried back over to Milly who remained lying flat on the ground. "Milly? Milly? I said. I lifted her upper half up closer to me. I cradled the back of her head, and lightly tapped her cheek. "Milly, come on, come on."

Her eyes slowly opened and joy washed over her face in the pale moonlight. She raised her left hand and brushed the back of her fingers against my cheek. I lifted her shirt to check the stab wound under the spot of blood and saw nothing, her stomach was smooth and flat as if she was never hurt at all. I was overjoyed, ecstatic even.

"Milly you're okay!" I said. The smile on her face faded away and her eyes became watery. "What is it?" I asked.

"I have to go," she struggled to say.

"Wh—what do you mean you have to go?" I asked. "I did it! I beat Madam Maria, Meridiana is gone, we—I—"

Milly grabbed my shoulder tightly. "Thank you D'Angelo. Thank you for everything"

Milly became increasingly lighter as the seconds rolled by, leaving me confused. I looked up and down her body searching for any abnormalities but couldn't find what was wrong. That was until I noticed her face began to slowly turn blue and then gray, patches of her skin and hair began to fly off in the gentle wind. "Wait, what's happening? What's happening?" I asked.

"It's okay," she whispered. "We're all going to be—okay."

Microcracks had begun to spread across her face and arms. Her arm fell to her side, plopping to the ground lifeless. Her eyes didn't falter as they remained staring up at me. In her dying moments she had rapidly turned to ash and fell to the ground, seeping between my fingers. I looked into the pile of ash of what used to be her eyes, her mouth, her shoulders, her hair, now all reduced to flakes laid out on the floor. Tears ran down my face, as I sobbed over what used to be my dear friend.

Milly.

Chapter
TWENTY-FOUR

THE SUN

I walked down the familiar long and damp hallway again, escorted by two Eclipse personnel, one on each side of me. This time I didn't have my eyes covered nor did I walk with fear in my heart and mind. I walked confidently as I knew this escort wasn't on bad terms, since I had helped them after all with the Madam Maria case. When The Eclipse showed up to my doorstep, they had said Ezkekial wanted to speak to me.

It has been three days since the night I had put an end to Madam Maria. Things have quieted down since then thankfully, but even if it hadn't, I didn't have the mental or emotional capacity to fight any more. I've seen enough paranormal and demonic events in one lifetime, enough for the average person to question everything before eventually spiraling into an existential crisis. I rolled with the punches as stoic as I possibly could. Not dwelling on the faces of demons, the sounds of possessed people groaning in agony, not to mention almost dying several times. I was exhausted every way imaginable.

Soon after we defeated Madam Maria, a second eclipse team came to evacuate all of us. In the midst I was separated from Jessica and Ricky. I remember we almost all went to the hospital for various injuries, some more intense than others, while others didn't make it. I myself was one of the few who went to The Eclipse's care unit for my non-life-threatening injuries. But then again how severe an injury would have to be to be classified as life threatening? When I was admitted in the care unit I saw people with broken legs, blackened eyes and missing teeth strolling in the care unit. Even then it was a bloody mess that made me sick to my stomach.

Looking at everybody made me feel lucky to have only sustained minor injuries. Milly's kick to my gut was surely the most painful blow I took that night, making it hard to walk straight the rest of the day. A few cuts riddled the top of my face thanks to Madam Maria's temper tantrum and my hands, wrists, legs and back were also all sore.

Once I was allowed to leave, I went straight home and fell asleep. I haven't spoken to anyone since that night. Neither Jessica or Ricky has answered my calls or texts. In the meantime, my mind replayed the scarring moments of that night over and over, trying my best to make sense of it all, and coming to terms that Milly was gone. I was a wreck the first couple of days, so much so that I emailed my professors that I wouldn't be able to make it to class due to being 'sick'.

As we neared the interrogation room, one of the escorts pointed to the door, directing me to walk ahead and go inside. I stood in the door frame just before entering, and saw Jessica sitting on the table with her left wrist in a black brace, with Ricky who sat in a chair across from her. I walked into what seemed like a pleasant conversation between the two. Seeing them alive and well gave me a great sense of relief and fulfillment.

In unison, they turned their heads and called my name cheerfully with faces filled with glee: "D'Angelo!" Jessica hopped off the table and rushed over to me with open arms, hugging me tightly.

I couldn't remember the last time a hug felt that good.

I looked over the top of Jessica's head and saw Ricky pushing down on the table using it to help him stand up out of his seat. There I was able to see his left knee also wrapped in a brace, as well as his right hand which was bandaged. Once standing, he limped his way over enthusiastically.

Jessica grabbed my shoulders and took a step back as she spoke to me. "I'm so glad you're okay!" she said, as her eyes twitched about my face, examining the few small cuts.

"Yeah, I'm glad you're okay too!" I said. "I've been trying to reach you guys the last couple of days."

Ricky chuckled and reached into his back pocket, whipping out his phone "You mean on this phone?" he asked, holding up the shattered screen.

"Mine is no better," Jessica added. "Come sit!"

Jessica tugged on my arm and led me inside the interrogation room. I took a seat where Ricky originally sat, as he joined beside me. The room didn't feel as claustrophobic as before, maybe because the door was open and different circumstances of course.

Jessica tucked her hair behind her ears, and took a seat at the head of the table. "So D'Angelo how have you been holding up?" she asked.

I curled my lips in and nodded my head gently. "I've been okay," I answered. It wasn't entirely true, but it wasn't entirely a lie either. I'm sure my facial expression spoke more words than I had vocally. "Just taking it day by day, trying to heal up, you know?"

Ricky and Jessica glanced at each other. It was one of those glances where they were both thinking the same thing but looked to one another for confirmation. I could sense they wanted to say or ask something they were too scared to.

"I'm glad to hear that," Jessica said. Jessica nervously cleared her throat and continued "Do you know what happened to Milly?"

"Well I...uh—" I paused. I wasn't too sure of what I should say. "She uh—"

A hard knock on the metal door caught our attention, silencing us. Alan walked in the room and looked worse than any of us. His left arm was in a sling, a bandage was over his right eye, and his nose looked slightly swollen and discolored. He pointed to the chair tucked under the table, across from me and Ricky. "Mind if I have a seat?" he asked.

We all nervously scrambled with our words, but ultimately we implored him to sit and join us at the table.

"Thanks," he said. He moseyed over and pulled out the available metal chair. As he took a seat, I could see some of the gauze peaking over the neckline of his shirt, which was probably wrapped around his chest and torso. It was hard to look at the condition Alan was in, walking and moving about so gingerly. It was like looking at a once prideful king who has been knocked down, and is now vulnerable and weak. The fire in his eyes had burnt out and his deep rugged voice had adjusted to a softer tone.

"I know you're all wondering why I have called you in today" he said, looking at each of us directly. "On behalf of The Eclipse, I wanted to thank you all for your help in taking down Madam Maria and her possessed army." We couldn't conceal our joy for receiving such accomplishment and praise as we each gave a grin to one another around the table. "I have some good news and some bad news," he announced. "Not only did you put an end to Madam Maria's possessed army, but with Madam Maria's demise, many of those who were under Madam Maria's control have since healed from their possession and are in the process of recovering and returning to their loved ones. Many of whom were reported missing the last several months."

"I'm guessing not everybody made it," Jessica spoke out with sorrow. The joy in our faces diminished.

Alan put his head down for a moment. "No Jessica. Not everybody. We as a team have suffered several casualties as well. Some of the victims of possession didn't survive the battle, others couldn't survive the transformation back."

Jessica pulled her hair back notably in frustration and sighed. I too was bothered by the undisclosed number of deaths. I'm sure we all were.

Alan seemingly noticed the shift in our moods as he spoke out, breaking the silence, and catching us before we beat ourselves up too much. Alan leaned forward and placed his good arm on the table, balling his fist. "But!" he said, "I don't want you all to think too much about the amount of lives lost. That comes with this job. Jessica knows it very well—and she's only been with us for what, three years?"

Jessica never disclosed to me how long she had been working with The Eclipse. I could only imagine the things she had seen and the pain she had quietly suffered in the night. I tried to recall the times where she had acted strange in the past couple of years I have known her. Any sudden disappearances, or any odd injuries she had suffered. I wondered if any of her "Volleyball" injuries were really injuries she had sustained from her day job. Or should I say night job.

"But I want you to look at it this way," Alan continued. "You saved nearly fifty people that day—maybe even more if things spilled out onto the streets of The Bronx. If you hadn't shown up, many of us wouldn't be here. I wouldn't be here. And we all live to fight another day." He leaned back in his seat and sighed.

Satisfaction returned to our faces and the energy shifted in the room. I placed my hand on Jessica's shoulder, as I was proud of her. I wouldn't have been able to do it without her and Ricky.

"I have one more thing to say," Alan said. "Your friend, Milly. The one who did all *this*—" he said as he pointed to his wounds. "We haven't been able to find her."

Awkward silence filled the room as all eyes turned to look at me, begging for an explanation.

"I suppose she didn't make it—did she?" Alan asked in a sincere voice. Ricky and Jessica leaned forward in their seats.

"No sir she didn't," I answered.

"Oh D, I'm so sorry" Jessica said, placing a hand on my shoulder.

"Shit man, I'm sorry too bro," Ricky added, placing his hand on my opposite shoulder.

Alan looked down at the table as if he was at a loss for words. He remained silent, but I could feel his condolences through his eyes. I could also tell he most likely felt like an ass locking us in the room when we wanted to help. Alan gave me a look of defeat; as there was nothing he could probably say to make me feel better. In a short amount of time, he understood greatly how much she meant to me.

"My condolences, son" Alan said, reaching out his right hand from across the table. I looked at his pudgy fingers under the light hanging overhead. I reached out and accepted his handshake. "Trust me, your bravery and the love you have for those close to you, will not go unnoticed or unappreciated. I'm sure she is thankful for you and all that you have done."

Alan shook my hand firmly before standing up from his seat. Just as he reached under the door frame he turned around swiftly with one finger in the air. "Oh, and by the way—" he added, grabbing our attention, "we have a few open positions. If you or Ricky ever choose to join, you all seem to be a pretty good team." We all agreed, not bad for some new guys. "And if you ever need anything, D'Angelo, be sure to reach out," Alan finished, giving a light bow before disappearing into the darkness.

A FEW DAYS AFTER SOME REST, I STARTED TO GO BACK to school. The weather on campus was absolutely phenomenal, as if the universe was giving me a warm welcome back to my academic sanctuary. The fall foliage took over the campus by storm, with a serene aesthetic of warm colors. The air was cool and dry, the temperature wasn't cold but rather warmer than what you'll usually expect in the cusp of October, but New York weather will be like that sometimes.

The campus had a steady traffic of people going about their daily lives and responsibilities, with not much of a care in the world, and finally I was returning to that state in mind. Gradually the demonic cloud of paranormal secrecy over my head started to dissipate. I couldn't fully enjoy it at times with the harsh reminder that it had cost my friend Milly. Fond memories would find a way to trickle into my brain during daily activities, reminding me of her and the fun times we've spent together, but the unexplainable euphoric feeling of the sense of a brighter tomorrow would counteract the mourning and grief I was experiencing eventually for some reason.

Maybe one of those reasons was on their way to meet me at the gazebo on campus. I sat there waiting and passed the time by waving to a few familiar faces that walked by. In between each wave I thought of what to say when Jessica arrived, and how I would say it. Do I start off with a joke? Sarcasm? Do I play it cool? Even when the job is done, I still tend to overthink. Maybe it's just because I care.

Eventually the traffic on campus started to thin out and I could see straight down the tunneling pathway where the radiant tree branches spread overhead. Just to the left, I could see Jessica descend down the steps with eagerness. Her curls bounced with each step she took and her pearly whites visibly spread across her face. She clutched some of her school books tightly to her chest. I stood and placed my hands in my pockets as she briskly walked to me, giving me a kiss on the cheek.

"Hey! Sorry I'm late," she said.

"No worries," I said, taking the books out of her hand. "How's your wrist?"

"It's getting better, but still sore," she said nonchalantly. She placed her hand on my stomach, and deviously smirked. "How's your gut?"

"It's better, thanks for asking," I answered, chuckling. I knew it was a harmless shot at my slight dad bod of a gut I have. It wasn't fat, it was just a little round, probably due to the stress eating recently.

"You ready?" She asked.

"Yeah, but I have something I wanna show you."

"What?" she said, intrigued.

"Uh—it's a little surprise, come!" I said.

"Okay—what's it about?" she asked, following reluctantly.

"It wouldn't be a surprise if I tell you now, would it?"

Jessica groaned in annoyance. "I hate surprises."

"Since when?" I asked, looking over my shoulder.

"Since—tuh, forever!" she answered jokingly.

I reached out my hand for hers. "It's okay! You're going to like this one," I explained.

She reached out, clutching my arm, and rested her head against my shoulder. I walked her up the path steadily where I had the surprise at. I enjoyed the feeling of her warm embrace wrapped around my arm, the smell of her hair and the autumn leaves. All under a bright sun. There's some moments you'd want to last longer.

We passed by several buildings on campus, leisurely strolling as we approached where I had the surprise waiting on the floor.

"Is that what I think it is?" she said, looking up at me with an amused look of confusion.

"Yeah," I said.

She walked a few steps ahead of me and looked down at the semi-completed circle of white stones on the ground. "I thought you didn't believe it could work," she said.

"Yeah, but I thought about it. Since Meridiana was in Milly's body, how could she be underground? Now that she's—I guess gone, she might've returned to where she was," I said, shrugging my shoulders.

Jessica looked back at me, seemingly impressed at my intuitive reasoning and searched for wonder. "Okay, even if she has returned, you think the silly little ritual is going to work?"

I reached in my pocket and offered a handful of white stones. "Who's to say it won't?" I answered.

Jessica's face glistened with admiration as she picked a few stones from out of the palms of my hands. She knelt to the ground beside me, and placed three stones down completing the circle. "Alright that's it," she said. "This circle is kinda big."

I placed her books on the ground along with my backpack, kneeling down with her. "I thought we'd do it together", I said. We lowered our bodies gently to the ground, placing our heads inside the stone circle, laying our ears flat against the stone tile, looking into each other's eyes, mere inches away from one another.

I could hear the footsteps walking past us, I could feel the stares piercing my backside from different directions, and the murmurs questioning our sanity, but none of it mattered—only she did.

"Ready?" she asked, holding a fist just above the ground.

I followed, and agreed, "Mhm."

"One. Two. Three," we said in unison, knocking against the ground with each count.

The ambiance of the campus grounds grew still. The birds, the laughs, the train, the footsteps all came to a close the more I focused my hearing on the ground below. I looked up at Jessica, to see if she had lost hope with the effort of listening but her eyes remained looking to the ground. I grew embarrassed and was ready to get up off the ground and call it a day. I lifted my head and pushed off the ground, but Jessica snatched my arm with great intensity. Her eyes were wide with fear and shock, while still looking to the ground. Her brown eyes shifted to me with urgency.

I joined her again, pressing my ear against the dry tile, and focused my hearing. Right away I was met with what faintly sounded like a woman singing a low drowned out tone. It was a steady note that sent chills down my spine, as it was vaguely familiar, as if I've heard it before. The voice increased in volume, making me retreat my ear slightly.

"Wait—wait," I said. I wasn't sure if I was imagining it, or if Jessica was experiencing the same thing as I was.

"Shh!" Jessica cut me off.

I placed my ear back to the ground quickly, picking up where the voice left off. The beautiful note began switching between higher and more softer vocals, into what sounded like a one-woman performance down below. No words were directly sung, yet I understood her message perfectly. She was happy, she was at peace, she was and above all thankful. Her voice echoed through the dimensions of life and death and vibrated through the hallowed grounds where we rested our heads. Somehow, her tranquil voice healed something deep inside of me.

I looked across from me and into Jessica's light brown eyes, seeing how she nearly wept at its beauty. It was as if this song, this performance, was dedicated to us in some way. I felt a soft touch spread across my hand, and fill in the spaces in between my fingers. It was a magical experience that not many people would ever experience in a lifetime. We enjoyed the vibrant sounds, like two spectators within a large opera house, being serenaded by a voice incomprehensibly out of this world.

Chapter
TWENTY-FIVE

UNTIL DUSK

The vibrant leaves fell to the ground, painting the sidewalks. Soon after, snow would follow and blanket the sidewalks inch by inch. Even on the bright and sunny days, the air would be relentlessly cold and painful without the proper attire. Weather in January would bring out the bitter blasts of wind.

Winter was never my favorite season, especially at its freezing temperatures, but this winter wasn't so bad, maybe because Jessica and I were in our honeymoon stage at the time. The last few months were filled with joyous occasions that we had spent together. I spent Halloween with Jessica, she dressed up as Starfire and I was Robin. For Thanksgiving, she came over and spent it with me and my grandma.

She even came over the day prior and my grandma taught her how to make baked macaroni and cheese. From matching PJs for Christmas to sharing a New Years kiss, the winter season was one to remember and cherish.

Jessica and The Eclipse didn't have any supernatural or demonic trouble that called for their attention after the whole Madam Maria thing. Thank goodness because many of the members still needed to heal from that battle. Maybe it was too cold for evil to poke its head out from the shadows.

Not only did my relationship with Jessica flourish, but by some miracle, my grandmother's vision began to return as well. When she began to see again, not a day had gone without her smiling ear to ear. She spent her days reading, coloring, and looking out the window. Before losing her eyesight she used to love placing bird seed in her windowsill garden, and it looks like she has returned to doing it. Recently she'd been getting mostly pigeons and mourning doves, stopping by out her window.

Ricky keeps in contact with me and Jessica. He actually took up Alan's offer and started working with The Eclipse under an "Engineering Internship Position." I don't think Ricky would've taken the opportunity if it hadn't been located in Florida. Apparently, there's a research group down there in search of a few cryptids such as the skunk ape, and the chupacabra. So far he said it's fun and pretty safe since they're chasing nothing but rumors and myths, we'll see how much of that remains true.

I'd be lying if I said I haven't thought about Milly from time to time. The image of her body deteriorating into ash and flying away in the wind. Some mutual friends of ours asked about her disappearance and I just told them that I haven't seen or heard from her either. Her disappearing out of the blue wasn't totally out of her wheelhouse.

I haven't told Jessica this but I've been having some dreams about Milly, some more vivid than others. One recurring dream I would have would be the one where we would sit on the staircase of my building, much like how we used to do as kids. I don't remember the exact words, or the topic of the conversation for that matter, yet it sometimes feels so real. Even in the brief moments where I'm able to catch myself dreaming, and begin lucid dreaming, I'm able to find her, somewhere hidden around a corner, or as a spectator in the back, silently watching me.

Even during the holiday season sometimes I would go visit Milly with her family, or she'd come over to spend it with mine, especially New Years, or swapping Christmas gifts. At the very least a text or call, but this year—nothing.

For a moment, she might've been the queen of nightmares, but she had always been the girl of my dreams — flaws and all. I like to think, maybe in another life, maybe things would've ended differently between us.

I was happy with where I was in life. I would say my life tipped over during the previous fall season, but that would be an understatement. As I looked forward to the new school semester, ready for a fresh start, I knew I wasn't the same man I was last year. I did have an ominous feeling of being watched every so often. Call it what you may, whether it be paranoia, instinct or intuition.

Little did I know, the world that I've stepped into was only expanding, expanding into a deep dark ocean that I was thrown into, and have drifted deeper and deeper ever since.

A world where you either sink or swim, eat or be eaten. Most importantly, you either become the light, or be consumed by darkness. Thankfully I had some help looking out for me. Some by my side, and some hidden within the dark. Far enough to be out of reach, but close enough if needed.

Acknowledgments

Thank you for reading!

I want to thank my mom for always being my biggest supporter and believing in me, not just in this book but in every step of my journey. To my dad, thank you for your love, wisdom, and for always providing a positive light.

To my film crew, friends, and community who helped bring *Queen of Night* to life in so many ways—thank you. Your energy, encouragement, and creativity shaped this story into what it is today.

And to all of my readers and supporters—this wouldn't be possible without you.

About the Author

MICHAEL BEASLEY IS AN AUTHOR, FILMMAKER, AND creative from The Bronx, New York. He creates experiences rooted in urban realism, emotional depth, and the supernatural, weaving horror, fantasy, and heart into his projects.

Beasley is a Lehman College graduate and began his storytelling journey as a director of short films, including *Queen of Night Chapter 1*, *Chapter 2*, and *Holding On* which earned accolades across independent film festivals. His background in filmmaking shapes the cinematic detail and character-driven intensity of his debut novel, *Queen of Night and the Witch of Westchester*.

Whether on the page or on screen, his goal is the same: to spotlight underrepresented voices, turn fear, pain and even heartbreak into fuel, and tell stories that feel personal, magical, and unforgettable.

When he's not writing or creating, Michael enjoys horror movies, feeding stray cats, fishing, deep conversations, and daydreaming about the next big story.

Instagram:
@B_easy31 @Thebeasleynetwork

WATCH THE QUEEN OF NIGHT SHORT FILMS

Before this book, there were the short films. *Queen of Night Chapter 1* and *Chapter 2* are the award-winning supernatural shorts that first brought this story to life.

All are available to watch on Youtube.com subscribe to The Beasley Network Youtube channel for more. Like, comment, and subscribe!

Queen of Night - Short Horror Film

Best friends, D'Angelo and Milly, come back from a witch ritual gone wrong. D'Angelo must now come face to face with Milly, who is now possessed by a succubus demon. The battle of the pure and the unholy ignites! Will love triumph over lust? Or shall the forces of evil have the last laugh?

Queen of Night Chapter 2 - Short Horror Film

A pizza night with best friends, D'Angelo and Milly turns into chaos as the Queen of Night is targeted by Demon Hunters. In this Chapter, worlds collide and friendships are tested, who will survive the night?